MW01701514

The Glass Vase

Annette Stephenson

Acknowledgements

This book is dedicated to those who have lost loved ones from injustice and unthinkable loss. Dealing with the pain and an empty heart takes time. While the ache is evident, so is the love and tender compassion.

To my husband, who is my strength and support during the writing process. To my family and my children, Oliver, Jacob, Kamara. To my seven grandchildren. You make me feel truly blessed.

To all my readers who love a relatable and heartfelt story, thank you for enjoying my words.

I have been writing stories since I was very young, around age 10. I have always had a big imagination for stories and characters that touch my heart and find a way to give hope. When I fell in love for the first time, he became the one I would give all my devotion to. Each story has a meaning and a ray of hope with better days to come. As hard as it is to lose someone due to tragedy, this story motivates us to hold on to the ones we love and we are thankful they can be loved by us.

The Glass Vase

Prologue

Bailee grabbed her keys as she prepared to leave for her trip. Both bags were on the bed ready to go and the ticket lay on the table in the entry. She looked at herself in the mirror one last time before locking the door. Bailee intentionally packed light, knowing she wouldn't be away long. She settled into the taxi and looked at the letter one more time. She was headed for New York.

It was September 11, 2022, twenty-one years after the worst disaster in US history. The day those secure buildings fell to their helpless ruins, so did she. How could she hold her head up through the pain of 9/11? She recalled when her own circumstances were equally disastrous. Reflecting, Bailee sat in solace as each mile brought her closer to her destination. She missed their humorous conversations, sharing their joys and pains together. All Bailee had left were memories of cherished moments with her best friend and older sister. Since 2011, Bailee and her family have attended the memorial where The World Trade Center once stood tall. After all these years, it's still her routine to honor the one she loved.

Bailee and Jen were loved. It wasn't that their home started out dysfunctional or depressing. They had a good life together, growing up in a loving household. Playful times and laughter were all they ever knew as children. They thought little of pain or the possibility of separation. Unfortunately, both happened through no fault of their own.

One beloved parent left Bailee's side and it took a toll on her and everyone in their home. How could a family go on losing what they worked so hard to build? She tried to rely on her sister for support. No matter how hard she tried, she could not pull her father out of the dark place he went into when his wife departed. That was the day the light went out in his heart. His joy and laughter instantly disappeared. His love, Caryn, must have taken it with her. He felt abandoned beyond hope until the loss of his daughter Jen further complicated everything. Only his youngest daughter remained.

Alone, Bailee worked tirelessly to bring her father back. Her desire was to help him regain his strength through love and patience. She also needed the love she lost. A sister's passing was a devastating blow to her heart, and it came with relentless sadness. When would her pain diminish? It made little sense that her father would separate himself from the remnants of his family. She needed him more than ever. How could Bailee find the key to bringing her father back to life and get the love a daughter desperately needed?

Honking horns disrupted her thoughts as the taxi swung in. Near the curb, she shook off her consternation and grabbed for her overnight bag. Inside was the precious journal. It contained the writings of her sister's inner thoughts and an obscure meaning behind the glass vase sitting in the window of Jen's small New York apartment. With the rest of her luggage in tow, she turned and entered the airport. It was a special trip she took each year in remembrance of that fateful day. She felt like she never took enough trips to New York. After all, her best friend had lived there. She looked at the schedule to find that she arrived early. Waiting among the busy travelers before boarding gave her time to reflect.

Things were good. There was love, there was closeness, there was family. Someone was always there for support. Bailee was known for her positive and helpful nature. Her life had started out with so much promise until disastrous events tested her optimism. Somehow after the losses, Bailee was going to have to make it on her own. Who would she lean on when things became too much? As she became aware of a void developing within her, how could she fill it? Needing love, she might find help, from the woman who seemed to rescue her own sister from further pain.

Chapter 1

Heartbeats

Luggage beside her, she closed her eyes and put herself in the backyard of her childhood home. She remembered her mother's garden blooming wildly during spring. Bailee loved how the flowers dressed up her mother's favorite corner where hummingbirds surrounded their colorful canvas filled with nectar. Her sister Jen, loved blowing bubbles and watching them float into shimmering prisms of purple and blue. Bailee tried to catch them with her hands as Jen waved them away. Caryn cherished her daughters. She could see that her girls had that special friendship that would grow with every year. They would always have each other. Sitting under the shade, she knew she could not join in their playtime like before. She still appeared young and lovely, but time had taken a toll on her body. She was fair skinned with freckled cheeks and auburn hair that beautifully danced in the wind. What had slowed her down?

Her girls seemed to know about her health. She believed they were enjoying their playtime; however, they were also putting on a show for her. Bailee glanced over at her mother, making sure she could see she was happy.

Caryn had tried to put aside that her condition would worsen. She knew about her issues before she met her husband, Chapman. She loved his unusual name and always referred to him as Chap.

When Caryn's mother died of heart disease at age forty, she realized the inevitable would happen to her. At the age of twelve, she learned that she needed a heart transplant. Her family never reached that goal due to modest funds necessary to sustain them. Medications and doctor visits were not something a young girl wanted to experience. That had always been Caryn's life, but she refused to let it stop her from living.

Chap stared out from the kitchen window watching his family, fearful of the day he would lose his beloved wife. She was the strength his family needed to get them through everything. He relied on her.

Caryn put her bare feet on the cool grass and slowly walked into the house. She didn't know how much life was left in her and she wanted time to absorb every precious moment.

As the girls played, Chap poured a cup of tea for her.

"They are growing up so fast, Chap," Caryn said as she sighed.

"Now, don't look at it so sadly. We did good raising them."

"I may never get to see them grow into young women. I'm surprised I've lasted this long."

"I know it's been a long road, but we have a good life."

Bailee had the same auburn hair as her mother and the curls bounced as she played. Jen was blonder with pigtails. Caryn would do all she could to keep the girls from the worry of losing a parent. Her eyes continued to watch the children as Chap spoke.

"You know how much I love you," he assured as he wrapped his arm around her. She turned to look into his eyes with deep emotion.

He still could not imagine any day without the love of his life. He was aware of the circumstances. Chap tried to explain to the girls their mother's condition. They could not fully understand. His love for his wife went deeper than anyone had realized. Getting ready for work one day, he looked at Caryn's clothes in the closet and broke down. She could hear him and came in to comfort him. As Chap was weakened from the reality of losing Caryn, he fell to his knees and held her waist. Caryn was wearing a long cotton gown standing in her bare feet. She stroked his hair assuring him that love would carry him through the hardest of times. Each year, Chap carried more weight because of the family responsibilities. He became exhausted with the growing list as his wife lost strength. He hired a caretaker to assist Caryn during the day while he was at work.

The girls became used to seeing their mother with oxygen tubes helping her to breathe. Bailee drew a heart and gave it to her mother.

"You don't have to have a bad heart anymore. Here, take this one," she affirmed as she presented it.

Caryn graciously said, "Well, this is very generous of you."

At night, Caryn would do her best to read to her daughters, putting life into the stories. She held both of them in her arms until they fell asleep. Both parents feared one day one or both daughters would succumb to that same dreadful disease. Despite that thought, they would take and hold any good memories they could get. They intentionally created a big impact on their daughters. All the love they received would be what they needed to become fine young women. That was important to both Chap and Caryn.

With Caryn being closer to her death, Jen could not take the news of her mother's health very well. She isolated herself, wishing away the pain of losing someone she loved.

"Why does she have to be in bed all the time?" Jen asked Bailee.

"She's sick. You know that. I made a wish and I believe she will get better soon."

"You're dreaming. Grandma died of the same thing. Face it, our mother is going to die just like her!"

"You stop saying that!"

Chap heard the commotion and opened the door to their room.

"Hey, what is going on here?"

"I told Bailee that Mom is going to die and she yelled at me," Jen explained.

"Now, why would you tell your sister such a thing?"

"Because it's true. She's not getting better," Jen said as she crossed her arms.

"She will get better. You'll see," Bailee defended.

"Girls, we've talked about the possibility of your mother not getting better. She needs a new heart and even if that happens, she still may not get well."

"I have to believe she will not die," Bailee repeated as her eyes began to show the sadness.

"No matter what happens, we have to stay together. Jen, there is no need to argue with your sister. With whatever time we have left, let's just live in this moment."

Jen walked by her mother's room and saw her laying weakly. She may have been just a child, but inside, she was angry and confused about what her mother was facing.

As a few days passed, Caryn was no longer able to get out of bed. She would open her eyes to see drawings that her daughter taped on the walls in her room. The caregiver was spending more time and energy helping her and watched the children after school. Chap returned from work and talked to Erica, her healthcare worker.

"How is she today?"

"She is struggling to breathe. Her blood pressure is lower and she doesn't want to eat."

"I'm going to see her."

"The children are outside. And Chapman, you might want to talk to Jen. She's been alone most of the day."

"Thank you."

As Chap went in, he first noticed how pale she looked. Her fragile hand reached out and touched his. He sat on the edge of the bed.

"Darling, it's Chap."

"How much time do I have?"

"Why are you asking that?"

"I want to be out of this pain, but I'm afraid to leave you."

"You will always have me by your side."

"I'm too weak to eat or watch our daughters. What kind of a life is this?"

"You are doing all you can do. I wish it was me instead."

"No. The girls need you. You have always been a good father to them. Love them always. Make sure they have your support."

Suddenly, he questioned whether he could be a good father to his daughters. "What if I can't give my best?"

"Right now, there are four heartbeats in this house. Soon, there will be three. They need you. Stay together and love them. Even when I'm gone, they can be happy because of you."

Caryn had no strength left to keep talking. Chap knew his wife was right. As she closed her eyes to rest, he searched outside for Jen.

Chap had built a small treehouse in their backyard. Bailee was playing alone under its shade. He guessed Jen was in the treehouse.

"She doesn't want to talk to anyone," Bailee announced.

"Do you know what's wrong?"

"She just tells me to leave her alone."

Chap made the climb and found Jen sitting in the corner.

"Hi, can I come up to talk?"

"What's there to talk about? Everything is going to change soon."

"What do you mean by that?"

"It's all going to change when Mom is gone."

"Tell me, how it makes you feel?"

"Scared, alone, angry. Bailee never cries about it."

"How do you know she never cries? She may deal with it differently. Everyone has feelings."

"I don't know what to do. What is it going to be like without Mom?"

"Well, we have to stay together so we can help each other. Someday, you will have to rely on your sister to help you through the hard stuff. Maybe Bailee feels lonely because you are not including her."

"I love Mom, but I'm afraid to talk to her."

"There is no reason to fear. Spend as much time with her as you can. She needs love and support too."

Jen threw herself into her father's arms. For as long as she could remember, Jen had watched her mother's health decline. She assumed that Bailee didn't care. No one could understand how she felt. Her whole family was being pushed into the unknown.

For the first time, they would be without what made life special. Chap tried to prepare himself for the worst. It wasn't easy to let go. Because it affected his work, his boss urged him to take a leave of absence.

A week later, Chap went in to awaken Caryn early. She was unresponsive. She had passed away in her sleep. He sat beside her crying silently.

"No, you can't be gone, Caryn, my love." He touched her face. "You held on as long as you could. It wasn't your fault you became ill. You have always been the best for this family." Chap was stroking her hair and touching her face when he heard noises in the hall. The girls were coming in to say good morning. When they entered they could read their dad's face.

"Dad, what's wrong?" Bailee asked.

"She's gone. She's at peace now." Chap continued to cry but tried to keep his composure.

Jen looked upon her mother lying there lifeless. She turned away unable to look anymore. She ran off and Chap could hear her crying. He ran after her.

"I need to talk to Jen," Chap said having emotion in his voice.

"What do we do now?" Bailee softly asked as her dad held her hands while she looked down.

"We grieve together. What would you like to do?" Chap asked Bailee.

"Dad, can I lay here with her for a while?"

All he could do was look at her and nod. As Bailee walked into Caryn's room, she just thought of her as sleeping. Lying next to her in her bed, there was silence but tears flowing for a loved and nurturing mother.

Chap found Jen hiding away, sadly curled up in a ball.

"Jen, it's Dad. Please talk to me."

"Go away! You can't help me."

"I can try. Please let me try to help you."

"Go away!" Jen continued to cry and isolate herself. He did all he could to help support her during her grief. Lilly, Chap's sister, came by frequently to spend time with the girls.

Bailee was ten and Jen was twelve when they first encountered the death of their mother. It came too soon, and the emptiness was deeper than expected. Because funeral arrangements made Chap uncomfortable; he asked his sister to do her best with what little money he had saved. During the service, he sat in front with his daughters clinging next to him. Jen got better at holding her emotions inside. She was not handling the loss very well. She kept whispering that she wanted to leave. Chap did the loving thing and just held her hand until it was over. Bailee was younger and observed her sister's brave face. Nobody knew what to say on the ride home.

The bed was refreshed with clean sheets and Caryn's favorite blanket. Jen was compelled to snuggle on the side of the bed where her mother slept.

"Jen, do you want something to eat?" Chap asked.

She couldn't answer. She needed to be alone and didn't want her father to hear her cry. Lying in the safest place in their home was all she could do. As he looked at her, he slowly shut the door.

Bailee still posted drawings in Caryn's room. Some were put in frames. She knew her mother was proud of her and wanted her to display her talent. Chap never cared if they cluttered the walls.

Those first few months were the hardest. The family stayed quiet in the home for a while, having very little to say. Conversations made it seem like they were moving on too quickly. Jen had so much she wanted to tell her father, but she always put it off. She just couldn't get out the words.

Jen continued to distance herself from her family and Chap felt the need to help.

"Honey, can I come in?" he asked softly.

She opened the door slightly and he put his hand on hers.

"I think we need to talk."

"There is nothing to say. I keep thinking she is still here with us."

"It's okay to feel like she is still here. This was her home too. I'm concerned because you hardly eat, you stay in your room, and you haven't really talked about your feelings since the funeral."

Jen turned to look at the wall to avoid her father's face. Her arms were crossed, and he could tell she was holding in her anger.

"How can I help you if you won't talk to me?"

"Maybe I don't want to talk about it! What do you expect from me? Talking can't bring her back."

"I feel just like you do. This isn't easy for me or your sister."

He touched her shoulder hoping she would turn to look at him. Instead, she moved away.

"Jen, you can't just exist. I'm trying to make this work. We knew for a long time your mother was sick. We talked in length about what we would do when she left us. What is it? What do you want to tell me?"

"Dad, I didn't think it was going to be this hard. I should have talked to her more. I should have been by her side every minute. There were no goodbyes or hugs. Like that, it was over."

"I know that feeling."

"No, you don't. You have your own way of dealing with the pain. You go off and want to be alone. I don't see any of us getting better. Can you leave now? I said all I needed to say to you."

"Okay. Please trust that we will be fine."

She shook her head as he slowly closed the door.

Bailee was listening from around the corner. Holding a new picture she drew of her family, she felt like she was losing Jen.

"Oh, Bailee. I didn't see you there," Chap said.

"I drew this for you. You don't have to put it on the wall."

"Your drawings always make me smile. I'll keep it in a safe place."

Chap could not see a way to get close to Jen after that conversation. She closed off her world and he wasn't strong enough to give effective advice. That was what her mother was good at.

As the months passed, Chap's sister thought it would be a good time to take the girls on a much-needed vacation. Lilly always put a positive spin on life. She wanted to bring them up to the cabin for the week. Life always felt better near the lake. Maybe it would help Jen open up and bring back that smile. After Jen continued isolating herself, Lilly found her in the woods.

"Does it feel like camp?" Lilly asked Jen.

"A little. I know it doesn't look like it, but I'm glad to be here."

"Well, that's what I wanted to hear. Did you get a chance to visit with your cousins? They're swimming over there together. Maybe you should join them," she urged.

The path to the lake had been there for decades and old white rocks marked its edges. They could hear the pine needles crunching under their steps.

"Do you remember when my mom used to come here? She was always the first one to get into the lake, then we'd all jump in. Before her disease got worse, she used to run sometimes. She had to take a break, but it never stopped her from playing with us," said Jen.

"Those are wonderful memories," Lilly said.

"Now everything seems like a bad dream. My dad just works and watches TV. We eat pizza because he doesn't feel like making dinner. He had to hire a cleaning lady to clean the house. It's just so wrong."

"I'm sure he's doing the best he can. It takes time to go back to normal. If you give your dad the love he needs, it may make things easier for everyone, including your dad."

"Maybe. It's been five months and I just turned thirteen. I'm not blind to what he's feeling."

They could see the sparkle on the lake as they got closer.

"It is hard, but you must trust the process. In time, things do get better. Let's go over by the deck and join the others."

"Okay. Thank you, Aunt Lilly."

"Anytime, sweetheart."

Jen stepped onto the gray boards that spanned the walk and sat at the edge. It was enough to watch the others play in and out of the water from there. Her bare feet could feel the cool water below. The ripples were soothing.

Bailee noticed her talking to Lilly and swam over.

"Are you having fun?" she asked.

"I guess. Why does it always look like you don't miss Mom?"

"I miss her. I'm also trying to have fun. I don't want to be sad all the time."

Bailee climbed onto the dock to sit with her sister. Water dripped off of her swimsuit and then between the boards. Jen gazed at the opposite shore looking for answers.

"Do you ever get sad?" Jen asked Bailee.

"Of course I do. I just have my own way of dealing with it. Earlier, I went over and touched Mom's name on the tree. Remember the one where we all carved our names? I couldn't stop crying. After a while, I came inside feeling a little better. Jen, why can't you be happy at least some of the time?"

"Lilly says things will get better. I'm not so sure. Do you really believe that?"

"Sometimes I believe it. You know, Dad needs you."

"He needs you too."

"Can you try? You'll see. We can be a family again soon."

Jen smiled at Bailee as she jumped back into the water, admiring her optimism.

"Why can't I feel like that?" she whispered to herself.

Jen pulled her knees to her chest and planted her wet feet on the wood. She watched her sister swimming and wished she could have her spirit. Jen finally stood up and walked over to the tree Bailee was talking about and studied the carvings. She closed her eyes to hear her mother's voice in her mind. She was standing in the same place she stood, taking in a special memory. That memory overflowed within her. She placed her hand on Caryn's name and whispered, 'I didn't get to say goodbye.'

Guilt overwhelmed her. Somehow it must have been her fault. A young teenage girl shouldn't feel that kind of weight. There was a lot that Jen was hiding from her father. The feelings she had for her mother were locked deep inside and she blamed herself for not expressing them to her when she had the chance. Jen hadn't realized that her mother knew how much she loved her. She knew how strong that love was and how she would feel the worst of the pain when she was gone. Jen admired Bailee for being the strong one, especially at such a young age. She opened her eyes and turned to look up at the cabin from the trail and hesitated to leave. Her eyes closed again, and she pictured her mother standing beside her. What would she say?

"Where are you now, my love?" Caryn said in Jen's thoughts.

"In the dark. I miss you."

In her mind, her mother was as beautiful as ever. Her red auburn hair flowed long with soft curls. She had a peaceful smile and breathed softly.

"I will always be with you. Think of me and I will be there." Jen imagined her mother giving her hope as she stood by the tree.

The image in her head left when she opened her eyes again. There were so many things she still needed to say, but it was too late. Jen wanted to come to terms with her loss, but it felt impossible. The next few years were not much easier. No matter what she went through, she knew her sister would not leave her side. Their closeness was the one thing she could rely on. If Jen could talk to her mother again, she would do everything in her power to say what being her daughter meant to her. Jen sat there below the branches, talking as if Caryn was sitting next to her. No one heard what

Jen had said that day. Later, Bailee would find those thoughts written in secret.

Chapter 2

The Escape From Reality

Chap had asked for a few days off and decided to clean up the landscaping in the backyard. The swing set and sandbox were no longer part of the place where his daughters played. Green foliage and bright flowers had long died. Dry bushes and trees were taken out and were in a pile. The fence was getting new posts and piles of dirt were standing next to each hole.

Jen had just turned seventeen. Bailee was fifteen. They were spending less time together. Jen would go out with her friends and frequently used her headphones to tune out the world. Bailee wanted to pursue a career in art with hopes that someday she could open her own gallery. She could envision procuring and displaying pieces dear to her heart. It was the one thing that made her mother smile. Meanwhile, Jen was making plans of her own.

From her bedroom window, Jen watched her father ripping and cutting out the brush that accumulated over the years since Caryn's death. After her mother passed away, she had little reason to be in the backyard. Why had her father waited so long to clean it? Was he also avoiding the backyard that Caryn loved so much? Jen just rolled her eyes and didn't want to know his reasons as she shut the curtains.

Bailee took over preparing meals and ironing her dad's shirts. She liked helping around the house and the routine became a normal part of her life at home. She noticed Jen wearing more makeup and her wardrobe showed a rebellious side. Torn jeans and a crop top was not what her father approved of. Talking to her was like talking to a brick wall. She would slam the door and turn her music up loud. Chap came to the kitchen to get a glass of water. His hair and face were dirty and he had debris on his clothes.

"Dad, dust off before you come in the house," Bailee reminded as she handed him a clean glass.

He wiped the sweat off his face with his sleeve. "Sorry, Bay. I figured, since I'm going back out, I'll be quick."

"I'm glad to see you working on the yard. It's weird not seeing all our childhood toys and that sandbox you built."

"Well, I'm making plans for this place."

"What do you mean?" Bailee put down the dish she was drying.

"I wanted to wait until I had Jen here. She won't talk to me."

"Dad, what is it? Should I go get Jen?"

"No, no. It can wait."

"If you have something to tell us, we should know. What is it?"

"Well, I'm selling the house. My friend Brad knows a family who wants to buy it."

"I don't know what to say."

"It's been five years since your mother died. I'm ready for a change."

"Maybe you should think about it for a while before making your decision."

"I've thought about it long enough. A smaller home would suit us without all the hassle of mowing the lawn and paying a high mortgage."

"We should tell Jen about this."

"I'm not sure how she's going to take the news. I don't even recognize my daughter anymore."

"Do you want me to talk to her?"

"No. You do so much around here and I appreciate it. This is my job. We can talk about it tonight."

Bailee looked over at her sister's bedroom door and a thought crossed her mind. Could there be a way to help her understand that their father was doing his best to make them happy? Bailee was the caretaker, or at least that was how she felt. She loved giving to others. Jen was holding back, and Bailee knew she just needed love.

"We can talk later, Dad."

"I better finish before it gets too late. I'll be a couple of hours."

"Dinner is in the oven." She paused and then called out to him, "Dad?"

He turned and looked at her.

"Thanks for telling me. I understand why you want to sell it."

"I love you, Bailee."

He left and she smiled. He poured himself into his work. His aggression showed in his hands as he yanked out more weeds and overgrown shrubs. He knew he was doing this to get out what he was going through with Jen. The anxiety of talking with

Jen about his decision was stirring up a stressful emotion. He just felt hopeless she would understand.

After dinner, the girls removed the dishes and Jen put her headphones on.

"Jen, I've asked you not to use those each time you help with the chores," Chap said.

"I'm not doing anything wrong."

"I know, but I need you to take a break. Help Bailee dry."

"Whatever!"

"Excuse me! I would appreciate some respect."

"Do you want me to dry the dishes or not?"

Chap took a breath and left to grab a beer.

"Jen, why do you treat Dad that way?"

"I don't want to talk about this right now."

"Come on. You know you can talk to me about anything."

"Talking to Dad is not the same as it used to be."

"Just try to hear him out."

When they finished, Jen headed to her room.

"Wait, girls. Come into the living room."

Bailee knew what was coming.

Annoyed, Jen asked, "What is it now?"

"I need to talk to you both."

Jen threw herself on the couch and looked at her nails. Bailee sat near her father.

“We never do this,” Jen said sarcastically.

“I want to discuss something important with you and I want you to listen, Jen.”

Bailee folded her hands on her lap hoping her sister would listen to what her father had to say.

“I am selling the house.”

“What?! When did you decide this?”

“A week ago. I already have a buyer and he’s in no hurry for us to move out. I thought we could spend some time at the cabin and be together so we can talk about a new home for us.”

“It looks like you want to erase my mother’s memory from this place!”

“Jen, please,” Bailee pleaded.

“I can’t keep up this place anymore. Your mother’s memory will always be with us. We need something easier to maintain and is affordable. Moving doesn’t mean I want to forget that she lived here.”

“I don’t understand why you are doing this! She lived here, she slept here, and now you want to throw it away?”

“I’m not forgetting what we built here. Things changed and I wasn’t ready yet. It’s a done deal and whether you like it or not, I’m selling it.”

Suddenly, Jen realized her sister’s expression.

“Bailee, why are you not shocked by this?”

“Well, I...”

“I told her already,” Chap admitted.

“You told her first? Wow, I guess I mean nothing to you. I’m out of here!”

Chap stood up to go after Jen and raised his voice, "Jen, stop it! I have had it with your attitude. This has to stop. You seem to think that I am not missing her or I don't care that she shared this home with us. I am doing this for us. Can't you see that?"

"No. You're doing this for you." She turned and slammed the door. They could both hear her crying inside.

"Well, that went well," Chap regretted as he returned to his chair.

"Give her some time," Bailee comforted.

"I've been giving her time. When is it going to end? I can feel it. I'm losing her."

Bailee put her hand on her father's shoulder and went to Jen's room.

"Jen, can I come in?" Bailee asked.

She just opened the door without a word.

"Are you okay?"

"I don't want to move."

"I don't think he wants to move either."

"How could he tell you first?"

"You haven't been the easiest person to talk to. You said you were going to try."

"Leaving this place is like leaving her behind."

"I can see that. But Jen, we take the memories with us. The truth is, she is no longer here. Everything we remember about her will always be with us," she explained as she placed her hand on her heart.

"Can I show you something?" Jen asked. "Since she died, I have been writing. This is my notebook. I put down everything I'm feeling just to get it out. For a long while, Dad ignored me and I just couldn't get close to him. I don't know where that came from. When I was fourteen, I tried to talk to him. He just wasn't hearing what I was trying to say."

"What were you trying to say?"

"I wanted to tell him about this guilt. I feel it so much, how I am affected by her passing and what it is doing to me. It's just so much to live with. He just stared at the wall, and it felt like he didn't care...so I stopped trying."

"Have you ever told him about this?"

"No. He has already made up his mind to move on. I have not."

"Hiding away won't fix it. You have it bottled up inside you and you need him to help you feel better. He's a different person now after all these years."

"I don't believe that."

Jen threw her headphones on the dresser and faced her sister.

"Bailee, you remind me so much of Mom. You even look like her. When I hear you speak or when I look at your hair, it's like I'm looking at her. I guess that's why I love it when you comfort me."

"And Dad? What about him?"

"It may be too late for us. I can't give it another try and I don't believe talking will work this time."

Bailee took Jen's hand and pulled her close. Jen returned her embrace. Unlike her sister, Bailee had so much faith and felt she could help. She was committed to Jen. Their relationship might change but would never break what they have built all those years.

Because Jen did not want to go to the cabin, Chap decided not to plan the trip. Brad said the new owners didn't mind the messy backyard when they purchased the house, but Chap needed to complete it to vent his frustrations. It turned out that physical labor made him see things clearer. He was still a loving father, but emotionally distant from Jen.

Jen was convinced he would do anything to move them out of their childhood home away from her mother's memory. So, she did the most desperate thing she could think of. She packed whatever she could into a large duffle bag and slipped out the front door. It was not discovered until the next morning that she was gone.

"Bailee, where is Jen?" Chap asked.

"I don't know."

"Her things are gone including her clothes."

Chap rushed to call anyone who might know where she was. While he was on the phone, Bailee found the note on her nightstand. Pain filled her as she read each word.

Bailee,

I'm so sorry I have to write this after we talked last night. I can't bear the thought of leaving you but I must escape the pain and find my own way into the unknown. I promise we will keep in touch. You are in my heart and no matter what life presents to us; I will keep the letters coming. I miss Mom too much and want a life of my own without complications. Don't worry, I am staying with my friend's mom. Tell Dad not to contact me. I need to do this. You were right, I have hid so much over the years and it's not getting better for me. I will never shut you out of my life. Maybe in time, I will trust Dad again. Please write me. You are the one person who really gets me. I wish we could both run away together, but he needs you. Love, Jen

Bailee felt her heart break. It was not a good time to lose another family member. It seemed like her father was slowly getting his life back. She wanted Jen to find a safe place with her fragile emotions, but her father wouldn't see it that way. On top of that, Bailee felt tremendous pressure to reveal where Jen was.

"You know something," he inquired of Bailee.

"I do."

"Where is Jen?!"

Bailee hesitated, fearing her father's response. He was sure to get upset and force Jen to come home.

"She's staying with a friend and her family."

"How do you know that?"

"She wrote me a note. Dad, neither of us know what Jen is really going through. Don't you think it would be a wise thing to leave her alone for a while?"

"Bailee, she's underage and my daughter."

"I realize that, but you're not looking at the pain she is in. She hasn't been able to find a way out."

"I know what that feels like. I've been there!"

"We have both been there. But I think it's different for everybody. It might not be the same for her." Bailee put her arm around her father and looked up at him and reaffirmed, “She’s safe where she’s at. I can encourage her to call you in a few days.”

He was anxious. Caution was required to avoid permanently losing her. She was close to eighteen. Chap still thought of her as the little girl who loved being a large part of his family. He didn’t want to admit it, but he didn’t exactly know what Jen was feeling. Her grief was different than his and it was obviously deep and intense. He couldn’t bring himself to just love her while she mourned the death of her mother. Bailee was closer to Jen and hoped that she would eventually come around.

That evening, Bailee heard her dad in the kitchen. It was close to three a.m.

“Dad, Why are you up?”

“I have thoughts going through my mind. Was I loud?”

“Your trips to the kitchen are not subtle.”

“Can I make you a cocoa?”

“No, thank you. What are you thinking about?”

“I wondered if Jen was always unhappy. Was this something I caused? What would your mom have done? So many questions.”

“We were fairly young when Mom was sick. Jen was always close to her. You had nothing to do with her sadness.”

“I’m not so sure about that.”

“Don’t overthink it.”

“Bailee, are you upset that I needed to sell our house?”

She looked around at the only home she had ever known. “Well, I’m going to miss this place. I know you need to do what is best for us.”

“It’s still new,” he stared off.

“What is?”

“It’s just like yesterday. My wife is gone. We’ve known each other since we were kids. The only friend that never judged me or thought of leaving my side. Now, my heart feels just like this house, empty. I don’t think I can go on and be the same again.”

The word *empty* reverberated in their thoughts. With his head down, Bailee could still see his tears flowing as he lamented the love of his life, the deepest love a man could have. She took his hand.

Like Jen, Chap was conflicted over their extreme loss of Caryn. He could see Bailee wanting to step in and heal her family but would never ask her to take on such a task. His fear was that Jen would never come around to mending her relationship and have to in live deep sorrow for the rest of her life. What more could they do?

Chapter 3

Who Loves You?

Chap attempted to talk to Jen many times unsuccessfully. She had become an adult and he knew he had to let her live life on her own. He would occasionally send a letter with a little money to reassure her that she could still talk to him and he would listen. But her faith waned the longer she stayed away. Bailee was happy to see him not give up in his efforts. The girls kept in contact weekly. Afterwards, she would reaffirm her father that Jen was safe and would not stay away forever. It made him less anxious. Bailee continually searched for ways to help work out their differences.

Jen admitted that it was a matter of forgiveness on her part and was getting better at accepting her mother's passing. Because of her unrelenting drive, she found a job, was promoted, and managed to get a place of her own. Bailee continued to live with her father in a small home that he purchased outside the city limits. After Jen left, Chap just couldn't be alone, so Bailee stayed on.

Each month, Jen would send a letter to her sister, mentioning how much she missed her and telling of the new life she was creating for herself. While Bailee was the artist, Jen was always good at writing. After getting her first journal, she seemed to take to it, but kept her writings hidden. She later shared her poetry with Bailee. Some of them were amusing, but most were deep expressions penned from a mending heart. There was an underlying hopeless nature behind them.

Jen often asked how her father was. She knew Bailee loved to talk about his progress. Many times Jen thought about stopping by to see him, but just couldn't commit. What was holding her back? What did he do so wrong that was upsetting enough to keep her away? It was a hidden ache Jen possessed and it wouldn't let go.

Both of the girls were getting older and wiser and their conversations matured each year. It was always good to get a phone call from Jen.

"How is the art gallery? Do you like being there?" Jen asked.

"Yes. I have been convincing Nan to hang some of my pieces in her studio."

"And did she?"

"Of course. Dad's place is so small, I have no room to keep all of them."

"What is he up to these days?"

"He's good. It got rough there for a while. He was so depressed after the move. We lived with Brad for those few months until he found a house."

"How did that go?"

"Sleeping on the sofa bed, not so fun."

It was good to hear Jen laugh. She then paused and asked, "I'm glad you have Dad. Do you plan on staying with him forever?"

"Well, we have been in this place for a few years. I just want to give him a fighting chance to make it on his own. We are all we have. He has never been close to anyone but his family."

"We are in our twenties now. He misses when we were children."

"I think most parents feel that way. Dad just has a deeper appreciation for those he loves and you know he loves you too, Jen."

"I know he does. I just need more time."

"I don't want to question your motives, but how much more time will go by until you realize he needs your love?"

"I know I sound selfish."

"No. You're not selfish. You had an amazing love for Mom and so did I."

Jen and Bailee could always hold onto that endearing factor with one another. It didn't matter what Jen was feeling, Bailee never judged. They had grown up and relied on the one thing that would get them through everything...love.

"I'm going out with some friends tonight. Would you like to come?" Jen asked.

"Thanks for the invite, but I have some inventory to look over. We have some new up and coming artists that want a crack at fame," Bailee chuckled.

"You are so dedicated. Okay, next time. Um, Bailee?"

"Yes, Jen."

"I love you."

"I love you too, sis."

Each time they talked was a treasured moment. It may have had something to do with how much they wished to talk with their mother.

Bailee had been working at the art gallery late. The owner was Nan Campbell, a former socialite who loved the spotlight. She was well known for late night parties among the rich and famous. No one thought of her as a stuffy woman, but someone who knew how to find the potential inside each artist. From that first week, she saw a twinkle in Bailee. When she brought in her artwork, Nan noticed how her artistic expression was unhindered. She observed how she mixed her colors and used each brush stroke to expose an emotion. The details told a deeper story.

"Darling, it's Nan. I didn't want to scare you."

"I saw you on the camera at the door."

Bailee was always fascinated by her. Nan loved dressing up for the gallery. It reminded her of Audrey Hepburn as Holly Golightly in Breakfast at Tiffany's. In her head, she could hear the quote, "I don't want to own anything until I find a place where me and things go together."
Tonight she was wearing white gloves and chunky pearls.

"Well, as you know, we have this art gathering next week. I ordered the champagne and the caterers will handle the food. It will be to die for! I would love you to display a few of your pieces for everyone."

"Really? I would love that!"

"You have been here for over a year now. I would love to know where your passion comes from."

"I guess I have always loved to paint. As a child, I used to draw so many pieces, my parents couldn't find enough room for them on the fridge or walls."

"Well, your parents must be proud of you."

Bailee just smiled. She wasn't ready to reveal the story about her mother. Things were going well and she didn't want the mood to change.

"Bailee, I want to show you something."

"What is it?"

Nan took her upstairs to a locked door. It opened to an empty loft. It was about five hundred square feet surrounded in white lime-washed plaster. Large wood-framed windows let in the northern daylight and reflected against the high ceilings. The hardwood floors looked worn and still held spots and smudges left by a painter from long ago. Her eyes widened and darted around, trying to take in everything.

"This is beautiful. Who painted here, someone famous?"

"Could have been. It holds a certain element of inspiration. Great works are born here."

"So, why are we here?" Bailee questioned.

Nan lowered her voice, "I want to know if you would consider this as your new home. I'm not sure what your living arrangements are now, but will you think about it?"

"Oh, I live at home. I would love to rent this if I could afford it. Is there any reason why you want me to stay here?"

"I can think of a thousand reasons! You are such a talented artist who needs to be in your element. I think being here will help you find your *je ne sais quoi*, your creativity. It's where you belong."

"This is so incredible! I should think about it first. I can let you know tomorrow."

"Take all the time you need. I'll put in a small kitchen and bathroom first. It will make a nice studio for you."

"Thank you," she repeated.

As they descended back into the gallery, Nan listed, "I have a few things to get out of storage. I'm donating some canvases and brushes to a school teaching kids to appreciate the arts."

"Oh, that's nice of you."

"It's my joy. I love doing it. Talk to you later, love." She swept out of the gallery with a whimsical flourish that made Bailee smile.

After locking up, Bailee stretched, took her ponytail out and messed with her hair. She was tired and ready to go home. Her decision required deep thought. She had been the protector of her family, the one person who gave of herself to keep her family from falling apart and helping them staying positive. At least that was what she believed. On her desk, she kept a framed picture of her mother taken when she was her age. It always amazed her how much they resembled each other. Her sister used to wish that she had her mother's red tones instead of the blond hair she was born with. Chap often told the story behind Caryn's beautiful green eyes and how he fell in love when he first saw her at the age of six. She captivated him. Their kind of love was rare and something Bailee knew she would never find. In secret, she ached for the arms of her mother to reach out again and hold her. But in her mind, it was her role to be strong for everyone else. As she stared at her mother's smile, she realized she should look for a way to be happy too.

The rent Nan suggested was definitely reasonable and Bailee had already been considering a place of her own, so this was a good opportunity. She hesitated, unsure if it was the right time to let her dad live on his own. Besides, it would be a while before the studio was ready.

Arriving home, she found Chap watching TV in his room. She stopped by the fridge to get a snack before going to bed. She washed and put a cluster of red grapes in a bowl.

"Bailee?" Chap yelled from his room.

"Yeah, Dad. Just getting something to eat."

"You worked late."

"We got an event coming up and Nan wanted to talk to me."

Chap turned off the TV and came out to catch up. Her world felt so much more interesting than his.

"What about?"

"Well, she showed me her studio above the gallery. Dad, she wants to turn it into an apartment! A place where I can live and paint."

Chap bent his gaze downward and asked, "What did you tell her?"

"I said I'd think about it. I don't want to leave you."

He lifted his chin, happy that she had considered him.

"Bailee, you are a grown woman. I know these last few years felt necessary, but I also want you to have a life for yourself. You have a good future in front of you."

"I've been with you for so long and I'm almost twenty-five now. I know time has passed. I want to be sure you are going to be okay here without me."

"Of course, I'll miss you. I'm not always alone. Brad comes over from time to time. Why are you holding back?"

"Because I love you so much."

"Just like your mom. She was always thinking of others first before she cared for herself. You won't be far from here. I think I'll be fine."

"Dad, I talked to Jen this afternoon."

Chap turned to leave.

"Dad, why are you going?"

He stopped to look back at her.

"Do I want to hear about how much she refuses to see me? Bailee, it gets tiring, you know?"

"I get it. But she asked about you."

"But?"

"She's still not ready. She mentioned you and maybe she still wants to be part of your life."

"I'll believe it when I see it."

"As much as we talk, I'm really not sure why she is still so distant from you. Something is deeply embedded in her heart and I still don't know what it is."

"Well, like you said, she'll come around, someday."

She suddenly felt like he wasn't ready to be alone. Her mind was unsure how it would play out.

"I can still stay here with you, Dad."

"No, Bailee. You should have your own place. You belong there at the gallery. I've saved every drawing you have made for me. The move will be good for you. What you do at that gallery means a lot to me too."

"Oh, Dad. Thank you," she sighed. Bailee wrapped her arms around his neck to assure him that she would always be close if he needed her.

Chap was trying to be as patient as he could. He knew Bailee had taken it upon herself to care for him and stabilize his emotions during rough times. They had made it together without the one they loved. Bailee's conversations suggested that Jen was not trying to be coldhearted. Her hidden pain was a battle they hoped she would win in time. It's hard for young people to think about maturity and what parents need from them. Jen appeared selfish at times but preferred to protect herself from further heartache. She had to rely on her own support. Was that the wisest thing to do? Jen's choices would ultimately affect her life more than she realized. She would be tested and experience consequences from her questionable decisions that put her on a path of uncertainty.

Chapter 4

Chapman and Caryn

Cherry blossoms showed off vibrant pinks and whites as the wind waved branches towards spring skies. Petals tumbled and floated into the schoolyard. Caryn loved gathering them together to make a small bouquet for herself. She knew they wouldn't keep long after they fell, but she didn't care in the moment. Pigtails and a pleasant smile showed who she really was. Chapman noticed her each day during recess picking flowers, whether it was dandelions or just petals off the tree. Sometimes she would gather a handful and throw them in the air and twirl, throwing her arms upwards. He watched the young girl and wondered why she never ran or played as the others. Why did she prefer to be alone? She did have friends, but when outside, she didn't play with them. What kind of a life was that for a beautiful six year old? There she sat, the little red-haired girl who found ways to entertain herself and looked happy doing it. The few times he heard her laugh made him smile. It was like music to his ears. Being in Kindergarten was a good place to be for Chap. Standing by the basketball court, his friends called out to him as he held the ball. He was looking at Caryn. His curiosity was getting the best of him and he could no longer just watch.

"Chap, what are you doing? Throw the ball."

He turned to look at the boys waiting for him and suddenly dropped the ball and rushed over to Caryn.

"Let him go! We're playing without you, Chap," one boy shouted.

There she was in her pink dress with white ribbons in her hair. He was more intrigued than fearful. After all, she was a girl and most boys couldn't talk to girls at his age. She had a pile of petals on her lap when she saw him come towards her.

"Hi, I'm Chap."

"I'm Caryn. How do you do?"

"What?"

"Oh, that's how a lady says hello."

"You're a lady?"

"I sure am. Would you like a seat?"

"Okay. What are you doing sitting here alone?"

"Well, I'm not alone anymore. I see you in class. Why haven't you come to talk to me before?"

"I guess I didn't know what to say."

"You're not having trouble now."

"Really, why are you here alone?"

"I don't like to talk about it. My mom asked me not to explain why playing with the other kids is difficult for me."

"Do you think they will laugh at you?"

"No. But some of the kids won't understand."

"I'll understand if you want me to. Give it a try."

"Promise you won't tell anyone?"

"Okay."

"Give me your hand," she requested.

Chap held out his hand. He opened it and she put a few petals in his palm. She then put her hand over them.

"Now, promise me that you will not tell anyone what you are about to hear."

"I promise not to tell anyone about your secret."

Chap loved holding her hand. When she released, she put each of the petals in her pocket.

"These are special because you promised."

"You really love flowers."

"They make me happy."

"Are you sad?"

"Maybe just a little. You see, I have a bad heart. I was born with a disease that makes me tired and makes it hard to breathe. I have to take medicine and go to the doctor a lot."

"So you can't run?"

"Well, not very well. I have to be careful. I need a new heart, but the waiting list is long."

Caryn was not aware that her parents could not afford to get their daughter a new heart. They managed to save some money but it would be too late by the time they could accumulate enough. Caryn's mother, Pamela, also had the same disease. It was a lot for their family to take. They never imagined their own daughter would be born with the same health issue. They made sure it never took away the quality of her life. Despite all that she had been through, Caryn was a happy child.

He wrinkled his face. "How sick are you?" he pried.

"The doctor says I may get to live a long time. I just do what they ask me to do and wait for a new heart."

"You don't look like you're very sick. I see you smile all the time."

"My mother says, "*Smiling is what makes everything better.*" Maybe if I smile enough I can get well without a new heart."

"I hope that's true for you."

He scooted closer to her and asked, "Can I have some of those petals?"

"Okay, but they lose their color and dry out. I used to put mine in a book to keep them safe. Sometimes I rub them on my cheek because they are so soft. Now when the wind blows the cherry blossoms off the tree, I gather them and just hold them."

"It seems to make you happy."

"Yep. It sure does."

"Would you like to walk around where the grass is?"

She agreed to walk with him. She couldn't help looking for dandelion seeds to blow in the wind. Chap had never thought about talking to a girl. Seeing Caryn's view of a happy life gave him a purpose and a new friend. It was rare to see two kids in school so young with such affection for each other. They partnered up for school projects and tried to sit next to each other in class. Many of the other children poked fun and teased them about their friendship. Chap always reassured her they were just words and that her presence made him happy. When Chap walked home from school, he used to step on the fallen flowers. Now he looked at them differently. He would think of Caryn when he'd seen them rustling above and sometimes gathered a few petals to carry home. He kept them in a safe place.

As the years went by, time changed so much for them. Throughout their younger years, Chap and Caryn stayed close to each other. High school was a special time for dances, football games, and pep rallies. Chap wanted the memories of his school years to be about Caryn. But she found someone special and it wasn't Chap. Age and growth changed things for them. She would occasionally wave at him by the lockers. He wondered what it would have been like if they continued to stay together? Was she happy? Did she miss him?

During senior year, their school was holding an annual dance. He knew Caryn would be there. He came with a date, a friend of his sister's. She was younger and just wanted to attend her first dance. He promised that he would stay until the dance was over. When Chap walked in with her, he could see that everyone was wearing their best. Standing by the punch bowl was Caryn. She looked beautiful in her white gown and long auburn hair cascading down her back. She turned and noticed him. She smiled. It was hard to see her with someone else. He walked over and grabbed two paper cups and poured some punch.

"Hi, Chap. I'm happy to see you here."

"I wanted to come."

"Who's that?" she asked.

"My sister's friend, Allie. She's a freshman and this is her first dance."

"Well, I hope she has a good time."

"Thank you." He gave a slight smile as he walked away from her, taking a last look.

"Chap?"

"Yes," he turned his head.

"Save me a dance."

He just nodded with a slight smile.

Chap refused to believe that Caryn broke his heart. He knew that as children grew, they changed. He always held the hope that she would change her mind and return to him. He remembered what she said the first time he met her. *A smile makes everything better.* Those words were marked onto his heart and it inspired him to wish for the best.

Later, the DJ asked for everyone to change partners until the next song. It was a way to liven up the party and get everyone on the dance floor. Chap's date danced with another boy and he suddenly found himself in the arms of the girl who changed his life. As he put his arm around her back, he could feel her long hair brushing against his hand.

She looked at him and spoke softly, "Are you happy, Chap?" They swayed to a slow song that made him feel his emotions come out.

"I guess so, but I miss when we were kids, what used to be. What happened to our friendship?"

"I guess we grew up. I do think about you."

"I think about you too."

As they slowly swayed to the music, he recalled that smile of hers. Before the music ended, he took out something from his pocket.

"Caryn, whatever you decide to do with your life, I hope you take me with you. You are always welcomed in my world."

The song ended and the DJ announced a change of partners again. Someone came over and invited Caryn.

"Excuse me for a few minutes," she said to the boy who wanted to dance with her.

"Caryn, I have something for you," Chap continued.

From his pocket, he took out three rose petals. Taking her hand, he opened her palm and placed them inside.

"Promise me you will take me into your heart wherever you go."

Palm to palm, he begged her to keep that promise. Her eyes looked up as she felt the memories come to life. She closed her hand and squeezed gently.

"I promise." Her emotions suddenly changed and there in the middle of the dance floor, she just stood there, looking at Chap.

He stared into her eyes and gave her to the boy. He walked over to dance with his date. Caryn couldn't help but watch him over her shoulder while tightly holding the petals.

When the dance was over, Chap found his date and left the room to take her home. Caryn looked around searching for Chap.

"Missy, have you seen Chap?"

"I think he's getting in his car to take Allie home."

She opened the door to see red tail lights slowly leaving the parking lot. Against her better judgement, she ran hoping he might see her in the rear view mirror.

"Chap, wait!" she called out, catching her breath. As his car disappeared she felt her heart break.

She had missed her chance. She didn't know when she would have the chance to tell him what the evening meant to her. She had stopped gathering petals for years and forgot all about them until that night. So many memories stirred up inside and she recalled when she felt her happiest. What would she have to do to get that back? Had she always loved Chap? Her deepest feelings for him were now resurfacing. In the past, it never took much for him to win her heart. It was never romantic when they were school age children, he was her best friend, always there to trust. Just seeing him again at the dance gave her the confidence that their closeness would last. She always saw him walking the halls at school, but she needed that to remind her of a special time when she was a child. She wasn't sure what had changed for her during high school and she blamed herself. He was loyal and faithful to her as a friend and always cared for her. She hoped it wasn't too late. Far off into the distance, she could see what he could do for her future life. From Kindergarten and throughout their tender school years, she remembered every precious moment.

All during the week, Caryn could not put it out of her mind. Without calling, she drove by and saw his car in the driveway. After parking across the street, she opened the iron gate and stepped up to the front door.

"Caryn, hi. Would you like to come in?" he asked.

"Uh, no. I just wanted to get these few words out. What did you mean that evening at the dance? What were you trying to tell me?"

"I shouldn't say anything. You have a boyfriend."

"No, I don't. I broke it off."

"Why would you do that?"

"Because this means too much to me. I want to know what you wanted to tell me."

He shuffled his foot and hesitated.

She continued, "Do you remember when we were six? I trusted you like no other. I'm trusting you again now. What do you want?"

"Caryn, I want to be with you. It's not like when we were little kids. We are almost ready to graduate high school. We are different people now. It might not be the same."

"Of course, we are older now. But what I felt back then is still the same. You have never judged my illness. You never left my side when I had all those doctor appointments or when I wasn't at school because I was sick. You were the one who never forgot me."

"I haven't forgotten you. Could you ever love someone like me? Could you put all things aside to give your devotion to only me?"

She searched his eyes. He was looking down and she lifted his chin to see him and his sincerity. "I can, Chap. I was stupid, stupid for not seeing what you meant to me. How many people find true love when they are six? I never want to let that go again."

He reached out to hold her hand. It was innocent, yet tender. Nothing more had to be said after that.

"I'll never let go, Chap. Never."

"You are my mountain. You really and truly are the love of my life," he said feeling confident these words were true.

They sat on the Adirondack chairs on the front porch for hours talking about those times when they were very young. It was not important to talk about the future. This was their time to reflect. It was truly priceless.

Picnics and playful moments got them through the harder days of her disease. A year later, Chapman and Caryn were married in a botanical garden. They were blessed with a daughter, Jen Bryce Collins. Two years later, another daughter, Bailee Carter Collins. Their life was spent enjoying what time they had left together, not knowing when Caryn would succumb to her illness. She was growing weaker as time passed. Chap dreamed that sometime soon, his wife would miraculously heal and run and play with her daughters. He looked upon the woman who used to be a bright-eyed child playing among the flower petals, the girl who danced with the wind. He could always picture her beautiful dress and long flowing hair. Where did she go? Every moment he could, he would hold her and give her the attention she needed to keep living. She would always reciprocate by making him smile and focus on life's positive edge. Chap believed that love kept her alive for all those years. Where would they be without each other? The years they spent collectively were years he kept close to him, like the petals when they first met, the ones he treasured by keeping them pressed in a special book. There was no greater love than theirs. Though their time together was shortened, Chap would never trade it for anything the world offered.

Caryn finally had surgery to help repair her tired heart. But her condition hadn't improved as hoped. It was a little more manageable. She could see her future. When her life ended, she feared leaving three broken hearts. Chap was on her mind, and she feared he would be the most hurt. He would have to go on without her. How did she want to live the last moments of her life? Who did she want to spend those years with? It was always with Chapman Collins.

Chapter 5

The Broken Jar

Nightfall came sooner than she wanted. Bailee sat in the gallery working later than usual. She had decided to take the studio apartment and was waiting for the finishing touches on her new place. She had a very close relationship with Nan, thinking of her as a mother figure. Nan never had children, so their friendship was a special one. Bailee thought about how much she wanted her art to hang in art museums and galleries. What would it be like to be admired for her expressions in watercolors, acrylics, and ink? Envisioning them displayed for others made her smile. It was hard to continue imagining her bright future when thoughts of her sister interrupted them. Jen was so far away from her emotionally. She hadn't heard from her in a while and wasn't answering her phone. Brad assured Bailee he would look after her father after she moved out. His company was good for Chap since Caryn's passing. She'd grown used to taking care of everyone. So, Jen not keeping in touch, felt odd.

Jen had been looking for a new job since her work hours were not compatible with her schedule. She didn't mean to ignore her sister's messages, but she wanted to separate herself from her family until she felt grounded. While standing in line for coffee, Jen dropped a receipt from her purse. The man in line behind her picked it up. One look at Jen amazed him. Her beauty piqued his interest.

"Excuse me, you dropped this."

"Oh, thanks. It wasn't anything important."

He looked at her up and down, observing who this lovely woman was. He had his hand in his pants pockets, trying to be coy.

"Do you live around here?" he inquired.

"What?"

"Oh, sorry, I shouldn't have asked that. It's just that I come here all the time and I've never seen you before."

"I'm not a big coffee drinker but I do stop by occasionally."

"Well, if I had noticed you, I would have said, hello."

She smiled and made a smirk as she looked away.

He was wearing a shiny pair of black slacks held up by leather suspenders. Below, leather wingtips spoke the language of money.

"Are you using a line to talk to me?" she asked. Her arms crossed but were betrayed by her half smile."

"Is it working? I'm Jason."

"Jen Collins. You do come here often so does that mean that you work close by?"

"I work for a marketing team just around the corner. We just added a new business and we're looking for new recruits."

"So, you're hiring?"

"We are. Are you looking for a job?"

"I have carpal tunnel just filling out applications and getting rejected."

"What did you used to do?"

"I was a receptionist at a law firm. My boss wanted me to be a paralegal, but it wasn't for me."

"Well, I think we can get you a position at our place. Why don't you come by and talk to me or Ben, he's my partner in the business."

"I have absolutely no experience in marketing. I'm afraid I would just weigh your business down. Besides, what's the catch? Flirting with me is not a good way to win my trust."

"I couldn't help myself. My apologies. No, really, I think you are right for the job. If you're trained by the right person, you can go far with it. Here's my card. When you get a chance, come by and let's talk. The pay is very good and you can start right away."

"I guess it couldn't hurt to try it out or I could just say no."

"Well, I hope you don't say, no."

The customer in front stepped to the side. It was her turn to give the barista her order. Jason was at the counter and took another look at her. He paid for his coffee and proceeded to leave with his order in hand.

While she waited, her mind had thoughts of curiosity thinking about a new career. She reached to grab her cup and turned to find Jason watching her as he went for the exit.

She waved and shouted, "Okay, Jason. I'll see you later. I'll take your offer."

"I'm looking forward to it. Nice meeting you."

She thought about how nice he seemed. She was amused by his charm and demeanor. She didn't think it was hasty to take his offer right away. It suddenly felt right. But was this the opportunity she was hoping for? She sat in the café to drink her coffee and took a look at his business card. She wasn't sure what this job would offer her or if this was something she should pass on. There was no other way to know unless she explored it.

Jen found the building address on the card. Their office was on the 9th floor. She stepped in the elevator. The doors slid open and she saw the silver sign by the door. *Mason and Thomas Marketing Team.* She pushed open the glass doors and entered the lobby. Its ceilings were high and it smelled new. The receptionist behind a long counter noticed Jen and acknowledged her.

"Can I help you?" she asked.

"I'm Jen and I'm here to see Jason."

"Jen Collins? He's expecting you. Third door from the left."

"Thank you."

Around the corner were dozens of employees at their computers. At the end was a plate glass window overlooking the city. It was almost overwhelming. The third door was made entirely of glass. She could see him behind his black desk. He was on the phone when he waved her in. She sat down and he wrapped up his conversation.

"Well, you made it." he smiled.

"You sounded very convincing. Maybe I should see what it's all about before I make any decisions."

"Fair enough."

He explained how she would be trained and what her duties would be. Her office would be right across the aisle from his. She looked over her application as she listened to him speak. She liked the sound of the position. Jen wouldn't admit it, but she liked him too. He was charming, using words that appealed to her. He took her in like he cared about her and wanted her to be a part of their team. All Jen could see was a nice man wanting to help her become successful.

"What do you think? You can say yes or think about it," Jason said.

"I like the hours and the pay."

"What do you like to do on your day off? When Ben and I started this business, we had no days off, literally. I really need to relax more," he commented.

"I go to the gym or I call my sister."

"That's it? Don't you ever go out and enjoy an evening?"

"Not much."

"I could change that for you. How would you like to go to dinner with me?"

"I hardly know you. Maybe another time. Let's see how compatible we are in the workplace."

"I can do that."

"Jason, I would love to take this job."

He stood up and held out his hand, "Congratulations, Jen Collins. Welcome to our team."

While he shook her hand, all she could do was put a piece of her hair behind her ear and smile back. Jen was relieved to discontinue her job search. She felt bad that she had put her sister off. She needed to call her and apologize. It would also be a good time to announce her new job. She had been thinking about her dad more and tried to get up the courage to call him. For some reason, she was still afraid to talk to him. She imagined him angry with her and starting into a lecture. Would he want to talk about her mother? Those were the thoughts that kept her away. But things were beginning to change for her. She took a chance with her latest career move. Maybe she could make plans to talk to her dad about their broken relationship.

"Bailee, I'm sorry I didn't call sooner. I was getting frustrated looking for another job," Jen said.

"Why would you be looking for a job?" asked Bailee.

"I quit working at the law firm. I didn't like the trajectory. I got a new job working for a local marketing company."

"Jen, that's good news. When do you start?"

"Tomorrow. This guy at the coffee shop offered me a job. It's on the 9th floor! You know how I feel about heights."

"Yeah, that you hate it."

"It has good pay and hours."

"How did that happen?"

"Oh, it's a long story. I'll tell you about it later."

"How have you been?"

"Better. I have been thinking about Dad."

"That's a good start."

"I feel afraid to face him. There is so much I want to say but I'm just afraid to hear the speech. You know Mom was everything to him. I wish we could have been loved that much."

"You really don't think we were? He did what he could for us."

"I needed more, Bay."

"This is your chance to ask him for what you need. He misses you."

"I have to go slow with it. I'll get there. How is he?"

"Brad has gotten closer to him. He needs the company. Dad still misses Mom so much."

Jen got quiet. Bailee could perceive that her sister had so much to say even though she held back.

"Jen, are you there?"

"Yeah, yeah, I'm here. Don't tell Dad I asked about him. I want to see him in my own time."

"Okay. Don't wait too long. Time goes by very fast."

"Sure. Talk to you later. Love you." Jen said as she hung up the phone.

There wasn't much more to say about her feelings on the matter. Jen knew eventually she had to jump in and take the risk. It was a big step approaching her father who had been waiting so long. Until that time, she would keep to herself. Like her mother, Bailee always encouraged her to speak out and reveal her heart. To protect herself from harmful words that might be too painful to hear, it felt best to ignore what she feared. Jen could not foresee that holding back could cause more trouble for her life.

The new job made her feel like she finally found what she was looking for. For Jen, her hard work might help her forget her loss and remove her fear of failure. Finding someone who promised to ease that pain may or may not be right for her. Jen never knew at the time that this man was broken, having a crack that would be a danger to anyone who fell for the narcissistic personality, a cunning abuser. That person was Jason Thomas.

Chapter 6

The Trap

Things seemed to be going well for Jen and her new job. She was calling Bailee more and sounded happy. She had settled into a routine that suited her. Jason was doing so much for Jen and it flattered her. She liked the attention and developed some feelings for him. They would occasionally have coffee together, talk on the phone and flirt with each other. Everyone at the office could see they were starting a relationship. At the end of the day, Jason approached Jen to talk.

"You are a real good fit for this place," he complimented.

"I do love working here."

"What else do you love?" He stroked her cheek as he spoke to her.

"What do you mean?"

"Jen, it's obvious you have feelings for me. There's just something between us that feels right. Don't you feel it?"

"Well, yes. I mean, I do like you and we work well together."

"Jen, what I'm asking is, do you want more than a friendship with me?"

"I would, but we work together. Wouldn't that seem strange?"

"How long have you been working here? Four months? I think everyone here can see we have something."

He pulled her close to him and looked deeply into her eyes.

"Jen, I want more and I know you do too."

She couldn't help but kiss him and admit she had fallen for him.

"You won't regret it. I can make you happy," he whispered near her ear.

"I believe you. Jason, don't hurt me. If this isn't what you want, don't lead me on."

"Why wouldn't it work out? Don't worry. I have big plans for us." He wanted to change the mood, so he made a suggestion.

"Now, how about some dinner? We need to celebrate."

"I'd like that."

He opened the car door for her and let her in. He held her hand while he drove. They laughed during their conversation and Jen felt that was where she wanted to be. Jason seemed so considerate towards her and her concerns. Especially when she spoke of wanting to make up with her father. The months that went by were the best she had ever experienced. Ski trips at the lodge in winter time, getting to know his friends, and attending business meetings where she could dress in her finest. Jen was on top of the world, living the life she wanted with Jason. He gave everything to her to keep her attached to him.

Bailee thought she would give her sister a call. This was the routine that kept them close and Bailee needed to care for her sister's concerns.

"Hey, girl. Where are you right now?" Bailee asked.

"I'm heading out to my car. I am going to pick up my dry cleaning and run some errands. Let me guess, you called to have lunch."

"You know me so well. How about it? My treat."

"Sure. I have some news."

"Well, when you put it that way, I gotta hear it."

"Okay, I'll meet you at our favorite place."

Jen took an hour out of her day to meet Bailee. The two of them rarely got together since Jen started dating. They did have their regular talks on the phone, missing the days when they used to be closer.

"Why do we come here all the time?" Jen asked.

"Because it's the best." Bailee noticed the smile on Jen's face. "Okay, I haven't seen you in a while and you're smiling. What's going on?"

"Well, I met someone. Do you remember the guy that hired me? He and I are a couple now."

"That is news. Isn't it awkward to work with your boss and now you're dating him?"

"It was at first, but it's working out fine."

The sisters ordered their meals and got into the details about Jen's new relationship.

"So, what's interesting about this guy?"

"He's kind and considerate. It feels too good to be true. He got me this job and now I can see myself marrying him."

"Jen, pump the brakes! Get to know him better before you start writing wedding vows."

"I get it. But it just feels right. It's got me thinking that I should call Dad. I told Jason all about him and Mom."

"I didn't think you would be comfortable telling anyone about Mom and Dad."

"With him, I felt like I could express myself. He gave me this bracelet to cheer me up. I know it sounds old fashioned, but he is very chivalrous."

"I hope you're happy. Just be careful and take it slow. I know you want true love, but it's important to get to know him better."

"You know I haven't been happy for a long time. Jason may be the one I've been looking for."

Bailee's concern for Jen's happiness showed on her face. Jen wanted to ignore any doubts about what could happen or how she should keep from getting hurt. Bailee took her hand and looked closely at the bracelet. Jen looked up at her.

"What? What is it, Bay?"

"I love you, Jen. I may be the younger sister, but I want to be like Mom and make sure you're happy."

"I love you too. I'm happy. Really, I am."

Enjoying moments together was Jen's favorite past time with her sister. Bailee was glad that she wanted to talk to her father and take that first step mending their relationship. It was good news for Bailee.

When they had to part ways, Jen gave her a hug. There was no doubt their bond was strong. It would always stay that way.

After such a good day, Jen thought it would be special to make dinner for Jason and surprise him. She arrived at his apartment and started preparations. After thirty minutes, Jason walked in and was surprised to see her in the kitchen.

“Hey, what are you doing here?”

“I thought I’d surprise you with dinner.”

Jason did not look interested and threw his briefcase onto the couch.

“What’s wrong?” she asked.

“I would have appreciated it if you would have talked to me about these plans first. I gave you a key, but that doesn’t mean you can come here anytime you want to.”

“I’m sorry. I didn’t think it would be a problem.”

He untied his tie and it was obvious he was upset.

“Where were you today?” he asked irritated.

He threw his keys on the table.

“It was my day off, you knew that. I spent time with my sister. We had lunch and I ran some errands.”

“What errands? What could you possibly be doing that takes all day?”

“Jason, what’s wrong? You know, maybe I should leave.” She threw her hands up and stormed for the entry to grab her purse. As she opened the door, he walked over and shut it hard, then faced her.

"Where do you think you're going? You never answered my question. Where have you been today?"

"I told you where I was. Jason, you're scaring me."

He touched her face, stroking his forefinger down her cheek slowly and spoke in a clear voice.

"I don't like liars. Don't ever lie to me. As long as you are honest with me, we will be fine. Do you understand?"

She was quivering and clutching her purse tightly.

"Yes. I'm telling you the truth."

He was doing his best to calm down and changed his tone to make her stay.

"Jen, you're very special to me. I never want to lose you. You don't have to leave tonight." He altered his mood very quickly and smiled. It quickly melted her anxiety.

"I can stay." She was trying to hide the fact that she was still frightened.

"Good choice. I'm sorry. I had a rough day. I got into a fight with Ben."

She put her purse back and walked over to the kitchen table where he went to sit.

"What happened?"

"Well, I guess this is a good time to tell you that I will not be working at this office anymore."

"What?"

"I made some changes he wasn't happy with."

"I don't understand. Why did you fight with Ben? You two are in a partnership."

"I set up a new office in New York at the World Trade Center. I want to run our business from there. It will be more productive."

"What does this mean for us?"

"Ben wants you to stay. I already set up the office space and hired some local marketers. This involves you."

"What are you saying?"

"I want you to come with me. We could be together and you can keep your job alongside me."

"Are you and Ben still partners?"

"No. We split up. I am the sole owner of the office in New York. I'm glad Ben is out of my life."

"You want me to move to New York? I don't know, Jason. My family is here and I am very close to my sister."

Jason got up from his seat and cocked his head puzzled.

"So, you want to end this and stay here? I think that's very selfish."

"Selfish? This decision is something I need to think about. To move away clear across the country is not something I've taken time to plan for."

"I know, but this way you get to be with me. Just think about all the time we get to spend enjoying the winters there, we will make new friends, and we can be together all the time. You know it is the smart choice."

Jen could feel the tension rising in the room and she was uncomfortable, feeling pressured to leave her family.

"Do you actually love your family more than me?" he inquired.

"Why would you ask me that? I care about you, but what I feel for my family is different than what we have. I'm sorry, Jason. I still have to think about this! Forget about dinner tonight."

"Jen, don't leave!"

"Let me go!" She broke his grip and after grabbing her purse, she closed the door.

Jason became furious. He picked up the bottle of wine and threw it across the room. It shattered against the wall leaving its mark. He expected Jen to resist his idea a little. He predicted her reaction clearly. He had planned the best way to present it to her. He believed he could sell anything to anybody given enough time. At that moment, his plans seemed to fail.

The next day, Jen came in to the office and on her desk, were sitting two dozen roses from Jason. He had not arrived yet and this seemed like the perfect time to approach Ben.

"Hey, are you busy?" she asked.

"Just got off the phone. I see Mr. Wonderful sent you some roses. I take it he told you about his move to New York."

"He was upset with me because I don't know if I can go with him."

"Well, our relationship is over. I just can't handle his way of dealing with clients and how he does business."

"Everybody gets upset about something in their life. I'm sure he's cooled off by now."

"Jen, there is a reason why I want you to stay here. You are a good team player. Having more people to carry the weight helps me spend more time with my wife and kids. I've known Jason for a few years now. He can spark off in a rage when things don't go his way."

"I understand what you're saying, but I think he just wants what's best for me."

"I'm not so sure that's true."

"Maybe your relationship with him isn't good, but he really cares for me."

"I just want you to think about what you are giving up if you go with him."

"Is he coming in today?"

"No. He said he has some things to prepare for."

"Ben, I know you care. I don't think Jason would hurt me. This may be a brand new start for us."

"I hope you prove me wrong."

She got up from her seat and walked to the door. With her fingers on the handle, she turned to look at Ben. His face was concerned. Jen's decision would need to be well thought out. But her attachment to Jason was strong and she was blind as to what Ben could see. She knew of Jason's temperament, but that was not a deal breaker for her plans. She wanted to run it by Bailee first. By that time, her mind was already made up.

Ben stood up to look at the view outside his office, wishing he could change her mind. There was nothing more he could do.

Jen drove across town to Bailee's gallery. She walked up the staircase and knocked.

"Come on in," Bailee invited.

The apartment was quaint and very much like her sister. Nan had a contractor install a few more windows that let in more light and exhibited a nice view. When the city lights came to life, the night sky was simply stunning.

"This place is amazing. Nan is a generous person."

"She's great to work for. I am so happy living here."

Jen walked around the room inspecting her sister's artwork.

"Now, what's on your mind? You sounded like this is important."

"Jason is being relocated to New York. He is putting in a business in one of the Twin Tower office spaces."

"Oh, the World Trade Center. How are you feeling about that?"

"I am going to tell him that I am going with him."

Bailee was shocked to hear it. She realized that she would not see her sister as often.

"Jen, this is a big deal!"

"I know it is." She wrung her hands as she spoke.

"This is like going into the unknown. You haven't made up with Dad and you haven't had a relationship with this guy for very long. Why the sudden urge to go with him?"

"I thought about it. I need to be with him."

"Why? What is it, Jen?"

"Bailee, I love him. We will have a good life together and this is what I need to get what I want."

"Have you told him yet?"

"No. I've only told his ex-partner, Ben."

"And? What did he tell you?"

"Bailee, I know you love me, but I don't like you questioning my motives."

"I'm not. Listen, Dad has been patiently waiting for you to talk to him. What do you think this will do to him if you go away?"

"I'll talk to him. But you don't understand. Jason makes me feel like I can do anything. I am not confused around him. I know he loves me."

"You are a grown woman. I can't stop you from going."

"Bay, you've been taking care of me since Mom died. Don't you think it's time I went on my own without you always ready to catch me if I fall? I want to be free to make my own decisions, right or wrong."

"You're right. I have tried to be there for you this whole time. There is a reason for that."

"Not anymore. There is no reason for you to treat me like a child. I love Jason and I don't want that to change for me."

"Okay. Will you do me a favor? Please talk to Dad before you go. You owe that to him."

"I will," she conceded. "Bailee, be happy for me. I promise I'm doing the right thing."

Bailee couldn't say anything more. She just hugged Jen and hoped for the best.

"I have to go. I'll see you soon."

She watched Jen leave. When she reached the edge of the sidewalk, they both waved as Bailee looked out the window. She was heartbroken to see her sister possibly running toward a big mistake. But she had to let go of her protective nature.

Jen called Jason and wanted to come by. He wasn't sure what her answer would be. She entered his apartment ready to give her news.

"Hi. Can I come in?"

"Yeah."

"What happened to the wall?" she asked.

"A little accident. Have a seat. I take it you have made up your mind to let me go on my own?"

"No. I want to give us a chance. I came here to tell you I want to come with you. I think we are a great team."

He instantly beamed with renewed confidence, "This is a good surprise. I'm glad you're in. We are going to have an incredible life in New York. Just imagine all the parties we will get invited to. We will have it all." He was obviously excited.

"When do we leave?"

"Next week."

"I have a few things to do before we leave and I still need to talk to my Dad. We haven't spoken in years."

"Haven't you grown up yet? You need to exercise your independence. Can't you just call him when we get there? I was hoping you would focus on us."

"I still have to see him. There's a rift between us that we need to fix."

"Is this going to be a regular thing with your family? Are they so insecure that they need you to check in? I just hope you won't ignore us because of them."

"Why would I do that? I'm going to see him tomorrow."

"Fine."

He walked away with an attitude. He got up to get himself a drink. Jen was perplexed by his comments. She was already nervous enough thinking about speaking to Chap. He returned with a glass and sat next to her.

"Don't worry about me, Jen. It's just stress. There is a lot going on, but we will make this work."

The next day, Jason made a trip to his old office to see Ben.

"Well, what are you doing here? I thought you were ready to find greener pastures."

"What's with the attitude?" Jason asked.

"The only one with an attitude is you. I have a lot of work to do today and I lost my best employee because of you."

"Jen made her mind up on her own."

"Not exactly true. You have a way of throwing your words out and getting anyone to give you your way. She's a good person, Jason. Don't ever hurt her."

"Who are you to give me a warning? You were a lousy partner to begin with. It feels good to be rid of you."

"I have nothing more to say to you. Use the door."

"I will make a better life for myself than you ever will."

"Keep lying to yourself, Jason. Live in your fantasy world. Jen will see through you soon enough."

Jason's eyes widened. He walked over to Ben and cleared his desk, sliding everything off the table.

"Never come at me with your words again!" he shouted pointing his finger in his face.

"It's over, Jason."

Ben was relieved to see Jason exit for good. He planned to take him to court to remove him from the partnership. Jason decided to go on his own. The timing could not have been better.

With nervous anticipation, Jen drove through her father's neighborhood. She thought about what Jason insinuated. It was starting to feel like she was crawling back to her father and begging. Bailee had always convinced her that it was a necessary step. Somehow, Jen wasn't seeing clearly anymore. Jason already had his hooks in her and he was getting in her head.

Jen parked a house away and left the motor running. She stared at the house for a minute and she felt tears fill her eyes. Why was it so hard? Why did it feel like her father would use any opportunity to make her feel like his little girl again? She could not handle a belittling experience like that. She wiped her eyes and her hand reached for the gear shift as she put it into drive. With a heart full of confusion and pain, she drove away. She foolishly missed the opportunity Chap had been waiting years for.

Jen sold her car and most of her belongings to have enough money to get a place of her own in New York. Jason had left a few days earlier and planned to meet her there. Bailee parked and walked with Jen into the airport. They moved through the line to weigh her bags and she threw her carry on over her shoulder. With three full suitcases by her side, they stared at each other with tears.

"Bailee, don't be sad. You'll get me crying."

"I know you didn't get to talk to Dad but I told him you were leaving."

"I just couldn't do it."

"He wrote you a note. He wanted you to know that he realizes he has to let you live your own life. I want the best for you too."

"I'll miss our lunches and movie nights," Jen lamented.

"I'll miss everything about you. Maybe I can visit sometime. A better thought, you will come home someday and we can pick up where we left off."

"Yeah, that would be great. You might get to meet your niece or nephew when Jason and I get married."

"What a lovely thought."

When boarding was announced, Bailee watched her sister stand in line with the other passengers and she knew it was time for goodbye.

"Write me. I'll save every letter. It's better than a phone call, although I will call."

"Well, this is it. Take care, Bay. You know, I'll always love you."

"I love you more."

Jen gave the attendant her ticket and took one last look and shouted, "I'll take you with me. Two heartbeats, true friends."

She blew a kiss and went through the doorway. As she found her seat, she held the letter on her lap. It could wait until she arrived in her new home. What she would read in that letter would be the last words she would ever get from her father.

Chapter 7

For My Dear Jen

My Dearest Jen,

How is a father going to get these words out to a woman who is no longer a little girl? All these years, I wondered what you would become when you no longer needed me in your life. Without saying a word, I knew you missed your mother and what she meant to you. If I told you that I understand what that feels like, you may not agree. Only you know what your heart is feeling and the pain you are still going through. I am so sorry you lost her. What did she mean to you? Where does that come from? I would like to learn what it is that makes it so hard for you to speak to me. I want to learn all about you and what you want out of life.

Bailee said you were going away. Oh, how my heart breaks, as painful as the day your mother left us and what her heart went through taking her last breath. Tell me your thoughts. Tell me you love me. Yes, I am begging for you to come and tell me what you need from the father who loves you.

Why the silence? Someday, my wish is that you will come back to me. I left myself behind to give everything to my family. Because this is not about me. Does this help you to know how deep my love is?

Are you in love? I hope you find what you are searching for. The love between a man and woman can be powerful while tender. I met your mother when we were six and she was all I knew about loving someone. I have faith that you will come to me when the time is right. I will miss you, Jen. I love saying your name, the name I picked for you. When I held you in my arms for the first time, I knew you'd be my Jen for life.

Please keep me in your heart and mind when you need someone to hold you. When the nights get cold, when the light goes out of your soul, when you feel like giving up, think of me. I know you and Mom had something special, but she was a large part of me. I promised to carry on what she left behind for you and Bailee. I have worked hard to keep my word. That is my bond.

In whatever you do with your life, wherever you go, the memories we created will be part of what shapes you into the woman you have become, which is beautiful. No, these are not words to win you back. I am still puzzled by the silence between us. I never thought we would be in this position, experiencing yet another loss. You are going far away from me.

I am a father and someday you will be a mother. You will know what loving your children will feel like. I'm trying not to let my tears fall on the paper that I'm writing on. I'm trying to be brave and say how I feel about the blue eyed, blonde lovely I called my own.

Come back to me, Jen. Keep it close in mind that I will be waiting for you when I see you again. I love you.

Dad

Jen read those words when she got to her new place in New York. She fell in love with the idea of writing her sister and wanted to keep every letter in a safe place. In Chap's note, she could feel the weight he carried for his daughters. She tried not to feel the guilt, but it overwhelmed her again, even at her bravest. It was her biggest regret. Taking a breath, she put the letter away with her tears staining the ink, bleeding onto some of the words. On the front of the envelope, *For My Dear Jen,* was written in her dad's hand. She held it to her heart and then placed it in the box.

In the distance, Chap was going through some of the pictures of his family. He recalled what it was that put strength into each person he touched in his life. Caryn and Chap had a very good life together, so for Jen to separate herself from her father was out of the ordinary. All he could do was wait and watch the days go by until she returned to his arms again.

Jen kept an old picture of her and Caryn that belonged to her father. After her death, she looked through their loose photos and this one moved her emotionally. She couldn't part with it. Her mother's hair draped over her shoulder while her eyes were closed. Her mother was singing to her and she was intently taking in every word. After Chap snapped the picture, he noticed Jen shedding tears. Caryn had a beautiful voice. Every night, she would sing to her daughters while gently touching their faces. That image was branded into their minds. The reality was that Caryn was slowly fading and getting weaker but refused to let that stop her when it came to showing love to her little ones. Chap listened in and at times the girls would sing along.

With all of those memorable times to hold on to, why was Jen so resentful? What made her want to exclude Chap from her life? Jen had to admit that she loved her father. Maybe it was the way he handled their loss. She hoped it was more profound. Jen expected him to jump in and rescue her, to save her. She required him to do his best and let go of everything for her. A child wants to be rescued by a reliable parent. In Jen's eyes, the heroine had always been Caryn. It made no sense for the heroine to die and the weak to live on helplessly.

The letter seemed sincere and touched her heart. She believed he still loved her. But that did not erase his culpability. She blamed him. That was it. She blamed him for letting her mother die. Without hearing all of Chap's story, she would always believe it was his fault. She stared at the photo and asked, *"What should I do? I miss you so much."*

Time could heal all of it, or could it?

Chapter 8

Let Tears Turn To Ashes

The view of the skyline was stunning from the 91st floor. Her spacious office with large windows had been decorated to suit her taste. At first, she wasn't used to her new surroundings. The outside noise of the city felt unbearable compared to the peace of San Marino. To go from suburb to city life was a big transition. She finally familiarized herself with the ins and outs of the marketing business, which boosted her self-esteem. After a few months, she felt like she had adjusted and it seemed like Jason and her were living the good life. He bought her gifts, jewelry, and celebrated with their friends at numerous parties. Jen wasn't thinking about the modest life she had with her family. She felt happy with him for the moment. Everything Jason did for her numbed or hid the pain. There were times when Jason had too much to drink and accused Jen of flirting with other men. The argument ended when Jen put herself in a cab and went home. He always apologized and used excuses why he was so jealous. He would spin the situation to make her think she was to blame. It was up to her to do a better job at making him happy. That was his ploy. If he worked his emotions up strong enough to keep Jen with him, he felt like he had won her over and she couldn't leave. He was good at getting her to believe that he was sincere. Jen would cry after a fight and she would look at pictures of them during happier times and get hooked again, remembering how much she loved him. He played games with her mind. His goal was to make it look like she was at fault when the relationship strained. Jason was no doubt, controlling. He built his business with the help of Ben but felt like it was all his effort that made it a success. He refused to give Ben the credit for putting up most of the money. He left no room for failure in business or in keeping Jen. Being alone was not an option. As long as he could keep Jen by his side, he felt like he could take over and win anything.

Jen was home alone, admiring the jewelry Jason recently gifted her. She never imagined she would ever have such lavish things to wear. Designer high heel shoes, gowns, and bags. Shopping sprees made up for much of the sadness she went through. It was all smoke and mirrors, though. What Jason was putting up were blinders to take hold of Jen to make her feel happy with him. She could not see it from her side.

Jen walked by a shop selling stationery and unique office supplies. The store was not average. There were one of a kind letter writing pads, journals, and pens to record cherished thoughts and memories. It was a cute place and she was drawn to it. She opened the door to hear the bells announce her entry. The smell of lit scented candles woke up her senses. Soft piano music filled the background. Her hand stroked across some of the books and touched the papers. There were several jars filled with pens, paper clips and markers. She had no idea that there were so many options for décor to dress up a workspace. She was attracted to a blue journal leaning on the shelf. Its cover was embossed with the words, *My Precious Thoughts*. Opening its pages, she saw empty lines inviting her to write everything within. It would be her new friend to vent to. She never wanted to express her feelings verbally, but lately, it became harder to understand where her head was. Her ups and downs with Jason confused her. The notion of writing it down could help get it out and better understand what he needed. The clerk at the store approached her.

"Can I help you find what you're looking for?"

"Oh, hi. I love your store. I used to write my thoughts in a notebook and I think I would like to upgrade to a journal. What is your take on writing down your best thoughts?"

"Well, I think it all depends on the person. I, for one, love to write down my expressions daily. It helps to let it go and sort out what is real and what is stress. It may help you with whatever situation you are going through. That's how I use it."

"It looks like this is just what I need. I'll take this blue journal along with these beautiful note pads for my letter writing."

"These are very popular. Who doesn't like to receive a letter? It's like a little surprise in the mailbox. It seems like no one writes anymore. I think whoever gets your letters will appreciate it."

"Thank you."

She paid for her things and went to get a warm tea before catching a cab home. The weather was cooler and she was still getting used to wearing coats and scarves when the wind kicked up cold air in the fall. She recalled how differently she dressed in California. Would she ever get used to it? Each day was an adjustment of some kind. As she sipped her Jasmine tea, her thoughts went to a hot bath and a phone call to Bailee.

She put her items away and placed her new journal on the nightstand. She drew a bath and thought about where her life was going with Jason, often promising and other times, being unnerving. There were times when he partied alone without inviting her. He did not answer his phone those nights. Then he would switch and take her with him and show her off. She learned that she was not allowed to talk to other men without him being next to her. He clouded her judgment; she couldn't see the beginnings of a toxic relationship. There was always the thought, *It will get better with time.* It was a foolish thought. She had been with Jason for over a year and things had not gotten better. She couldn't tell her sister that Jason was becoming more aggressive, controlling, and jealous. She had to handle it her own way. After a bad fight, there were always beautiful roses at her door with a note that could melt her heart. She fell for it every time.

Stepping out of the tub, she wrapped herself in her soft, white robe and warm socks. After towel drying her hair, she went to the kitchen to get a glass of wine. Soothing music played quietly in the background. Jason was out with some of his men friends for the evening and it was a good time to call her sister.

"Hello."

"Bailee, it's Jen."

"Jen! It's been weeks since I heard from you. How is living the New York lifestyle going?"

Jen did not answer the question. She was holding back tears while listening to her sister's voice.

"Jen? What's wrong?"

"Oh, nothing. I'm just so happy to hear your voice."

"I really miss you. Are you doing okay?"

She took a sip, "I'm fine. It is so different living here. But Jason makes sure we stay busy and socialize with the right people. Although, he is out with his buddies tonight."

"Are you two having problems?"

"We have our fights, but so does every couple. He always apologizes for being upset with me."

"Why is he upset with you? Jen, if he is treating you badly, you need to..."

"Bailee, I'm okay. He's trying and I have to give this a chance."

"You sound lonely. Am I wrong?"

"I know you mean well, but you're being a mom to me again. Why do you worry about me so much?"

"Because I care."

"I don't need you to care so much. I just want to hear your voice and tell you I love you."

"You know. I love you too. Dad got out last week. He went on a fishing trip with Brad. Did you ever read his letter?"

"I did. I want to write him but I don't know what to say. I don't want to hurt him."

"Why would you worry about hurting him? He would be happy just to hear you say anything to him. Just write your true feelings." Bailee was soothing with her words.

"You know, Bailee, sometimes I feel trapped."

"Trapped? How so?"

"Like I lost control of my life. After Mom died, nothing has been right. Moving here with Jason, making it on my own, adjusting to it all. I don't know what I want now or where I'm going," she pondered, then added, "But I assure you, I'm alright."

"I want to believe that. I just want you to know, if Jason makes you feel uncomfortable, you can always come home. We can pool all our money together and get you home."

"Thanks. I made a new start here and I need to stay."

"Alright."

"Tell Dad I said, hello."

As she hung up the phone, she took a picture of her and Jason out of the album. She had a lot to think about and it involved her relationship with Jason. She gripped the corners and tore it in half.

Chapter 9

Canvases and Sweet Dreams

Autumn leaves coated the streets with their varied colors. The morning mist rested on them, helping them decompose according to nature. Winter was coming. Bailee had created several pieces that sold thanks to Nan and some of her vendors. She was finally making a living selling her art. One wall in her apartment was a collage of her works displaying vibrant colors. Nan's knowledge of her talent paid off when her art moved quickly.

"Darling, you are a hit! I have some good news for you," Nan said elated.

"What is it?"

"I booked a show for you, for your art. I talked to a friend and he has agreed to put together a show with you as the star."

"I wouldn't say that. I just love to paint."

"You don't just love to paint; you make them come to life. I hope your answer is yes."

"Is there time to prepare?"

"It's already taken care of. My dear, you have completed thirty fabulous pieces in storage and hanging in the gallery."

"I'm really going to have my own solo exhibition? I'm so happy. Thank you, Nan," she clasped her hands around hers.

"I believe in you. Someday you will get to travel and open up your whole world. Imagine if you went to France to paint. Even more could happen for you."

"I've never been out of the country. France does sound nice, though."

"My lovely, I've been there many times. You would love it. When you make it big, you'll go someday."

"After my mother died, I tried to move on by thinking about what she would want me to do with my life. She always loved my art, even the finger paintings I did as a child. My dad saved every one of them."

"She would be proud of how far you have come. I know I am."

Nan grabbed her handbag and gloves and headed for the door.

"Nan?"

"Yes, love."

"Thank you for making my dream come true."

"It's what I do for the ones I love."

Bailee was floating on a cloud thinking about where she was in her life. Unlike her sister, she had no one to share this with except her father. She never thought about the possibility of being in love and giving herself to someone. Just the thought of that roused fear in her. Thinking about what couples went through in keeping their relationships strong. Filing for divorce, arguing, someone leaving, or worse, death claiming their loved one. She never wanted to be in that place, so she stayed at bay with her feelings, not getting too close to anyone. It could never be as good as her parents had it.

Bailee invited her father to her showing and he agreed to come support her. It was a cool afternoon but nice enough to put the art pieces outside under the tents. Each art canvas was put on a frame easel where they could be seen by those who came to look or buy. Chap bought one of his daughter's masterpiece's and hung it in his living room. Many admirers got to meet Bailee and understood the expression of her work. It was good exposure for the business. Even if she made it big in the art world, she knew she could never leave Nan. There was something special about her that made her craft enjoyable.

Nan was a lively woman, married many times and widowed once. She spent many summers in Europe. France was her favorite location to find inspiration for her own artistic expression. As a young woman, she worked hard trying to become known for her unusual pieces. Some of her art was eccentric and off beat. When she started spending time in a cottage in the northern region of France near Normandy, she fell in love with the surroundings. She developed a love for its fragrant flowers, visions of white wines, and baguettes fresh out of the stone ovens. The picturesque countryside gave her the solace she needed when feeling lonely after her last husband died. She decided to paint floral landscapes, the hills and valleys with its birds and wildlife. It became her second home. Her vision was clear, she loved anything that warmed her heart. While she was there, she met other artists and helped them sell their work. It turned out that Nan was exceptional at procuring art for her targeted customers. Bailee was a breath of fresh air when she appeared. Nan could see herself in this young woman. They could share their losses and their strengths, always ready to infuse positive energy to one another. Those sweet memorable thoughts of France were brought back to her.

When the show was over, Bailee sold fifteen pieces and a few of the vendors asked about commissions. Nan never asked for a monetary thank you. She relived the days when she was a struggling artist and knew Bailee needed the support like she did back then.

Bailee credited her inspiration to her mother and father's close relationship. Seeing them love each other and display affection in front of her, helped her to put that on canvas. Even if it was swirls of color or the wisp of clouds, it often reminded her of them. She was naturally talented and her latest environment helped that along.

Chapman was proud of his girls. Bailee had grown to be a well-balanced professional woman. He was happy to be alive to see where they started and how they became successful.

He knew Jen would eventually find her way and would learn from experience. Jen was still far off in the distance. She had avoided events or changes like breakups and death. She was always afraid to have her own heartbroken because of the pain of loss. She held it in and it continued to crush her. She drifted away from her father, realizing her mother wasn't coming back. When they took vacations at the cabin near the lake, young Jen would find a special place to be alone where no one could hear her scream as loud as she could, letting out her deepest pain. Falling to her knees, she was moved to tears, missing the best thing that ever happened to her, Caryn. As an adult, she was still carrying that weight around with her. When would she be free? She revealed to Bailee that she felt trapped. She was trapped in more ways than one. To try and shake off that grip was just too hard for her.

Bailee sensed that applying the pressure to heal made her uncomfortable. She believed Jen could get out of the uneasiness if she tried hard enough. But that required a lot of strength, more than Jen had. Bailee always wished she had that super power to just gather up all of Jens's pain and throw it in the fire, rescuing and revealing her true colors.

When Bailee went back to her apartment, she noticed a bottle of champagne and a fluted glass filled with the celebrated drink. There was a note by the glass.

"I want to praise you for your talent and success. You are a force to be reckoned with and your artistic expression touches everyone who loves and displays it. Congratulations on a wonderful show, my dear! Nan"

It made Bailee smile. It was the most special day of her life. She wished her sister could have shared it with her.

She opened her mailbox to see a letter from Jen. She unfolded a beautifully hand-dyed paper written in Jen's unique hand.

My Bailee,

I love thinking about what it is you are doing in that beautiful apartment of yours and working at the gallery. I know it seemed like I didn't care about your art, but I do. I have never been jealous of your talent. I support whatever makes you smile. You were the best at what you did to make Mom happy.

Jason and I are working on our relationship. He made me a partner in the business and I have successfully added more employees and clients to our company. There are times when he is difficult to understand, but we are making it work. I've gotten over my fear of heights being here in this high rise. The view of the city is so beautiful and I love riding in taxi cabs.

Bailee, I think about the cabin on the lake, the one Aunt Lilly took us to when we were kids. Do you remember when we dove down to the bottom and found those old shoes someone threw in? We were putting them on and everyone thought we were disgusting. We thought it was funny. Or what about those times when we carved our names in the tree by the bat boxes that hung up high? We would look for dead bugs and waterdogs swimming near the shoreline with the mud squishing between our toes. Aunt Lilly called them salamanders. I wanted those days to last forever. We never thought about time or where life was taking us. It was about being in that moment, making a memory. I'm trying to make new ones. Maybe I'm reaching too high. We will never get back those years and that is hard for me to come to terms with. I want to be happy just like those days when life was full of fun and passed by slowly. Now we are growing older and I'm scared. I miss my youth and what we built.

I miss when Dad used to let us ride on his back like a horse. We would bounce up and down and laugh so hard. Mom would tell the horse to calm down. When we would all fall down, he would gather us up and make us laugh. We would chant, "Dad is the best horsey." I never laughed so hard.

We would take a bath and I would make a beard out of bubbles and even eat some of them. We would make up characters and play in the soapy water never thinking about tomorrow. It was sure fun to be a kid.

Now we are states apart, taking on the responsibilities of adults, whether it be good or bad. The innocence and the good times as a child are gone. These are the things I miss about my life. Dad stopped all that when he knew Mom was going to die. He gave up on us. He mourned before she was even gone. Why is it so hard to share how I feel about him? Why didn't he keep the fun going with us? I may never come back from that place. The aches may stay with me until I find a way out.

I gave everything I had to make it on my own. I pushed as hard as I could. I put the pressure on myself and caused my own fate. I want to break the chain and get back what I lost. All I can do is continue to live and do my best.

You were always there for me. The world will never know what that did for me. No one will compare to you and the sacrifices you made to make sure I was happy. Even when I was negative, you would make me smile and we would pretend we were on that lake reliving that same memory. You would hold my hand while you told your story. I will be forever grateful for that gentle medicine that soothed me and helped me sleep better.

Why am I being so nostalgic? Because for years I have been wanting to get back to who I used to be. I know you never judged me for being the walking sad girl. You always said there would be a way out somehow. How did you get to be so positive? I wanted to sample some of that and shove it in my heart. I want the passion you have. I want to bottle it and watch it sparkle so I can smile again. I have hope that I can get it back soon.

To you my dear sister, I say, I wish you so much happiness in your life. It's good to know you are the one person I can express my feelings to without it looking like a sappy old Hallmark movie. You truly get me.

Kiss the sky for me. Dance among the flowers. Touch the leaves before they fall, they need your touch. Walk the long mile where your future is waiting for you. Take me with you everywhere you go. Love every minute you are alive and treasure every breath. Most of all, never forget how privileged we are right now to have each other. I love you, Bay.

Jen

Bailee was without words living in those penned emotions. Jen wanted so much to safeguard her heart and she had it in her to be determined enough to get it. The letters that Jen wrote would be the most profound words she had ever taken in. Rereading them, she would cry and Jen did the same with Bailee's. Their bond was set in stone. It didn't matter what came between them, nothing was going to break what they had.

It was relieving to know Jen was happier with her relationship. Because it was so touching, Bailee decided to start her response early and work on it during the week. Her last letter to Jen had a poem attached to it.

Birdsong

The meadow doesn't hear the wind touch the grasses.

The brook's don't know they caress the shore.

The tree doesn't know how tall it is.

The ocean churns a lullaby for all living creatures.

There are no fences, no boundaries to keep us apart.

The bluebird sings a song only we know.

He swoops near so you can hear him.

I will be your birdsong.

Listen for me when you hear it.

Bailee didn't care if she was a good poet. She and Jen loved to express how their support helped them to stay close. No matter how far apart, two sisters had each other for life.

Chapter 10

Into The Darkness

Jen took in the view from her living room window of Central Park. The sight of new leaves and seasonal changes always gave her a smile. When the tea kettle whistled, she uncrossed her arms and poured a steaming cup. Springtime always impelled her to take a long walk. It would help clear her mind. Last night was stressful and what happened was not leaving her thoughts. She had grown tired of the jealousy and aggression Jason exhibited. She went to her bathroom to pull her hair back into a ponytail and inspected the bruise on her cheek and the swelling near her eye. She had attempted to hide it with makeup but it was only a slight cover up. For relief, she took something for the pain. Jen grabbed her hat, backpack, and sunglasses. She was dressed very casual and comfortable. She had come to hate the gowns, shoes, and accessories she wore when she was with Jason. It seemed so beautiful at first when he showered her with affection and love. As she locked her door, she walked to her favorite patisserie to get a warm croissant for some comfort. She kept her sunglasses on, not wanting anyone to stare at her. As she sat at the table outside, she recalled what happened the night before, when Jason lost control.

Jason set up a champagne party to celebrate the anniversary of the business. They were bringing in a lot of money and Jason was glad Jen was part of it because she was the one the clients loved and asked for. He felt superior because he was making more money than when he was with Ben. In his eyes, life was going just the way he planned it.

Jason had a limo sent for Jen. She had her hair done perfectly and wore a golden form-fitting gown. It exposed her beautiful back and showed her toned shoulders. As she came down the stairs from her apartment, she wasn't smiling. Shouldn't she be happy that she had dressed up to celebrate with the man she loved? She was uncomfortable. Jen knew what she had to do to prevent a fight. Jason emotionally trained her to be someone she wasn't. She was coached ahead of time who she was permitted to talk to. Otherwise, he would embarrass her in front of his friends. He was skillful at making fun of her, exposing her flaws and laughing.

He had recently begun taking liberties that concerned her. It started when Jason welcomed himself into her apartment without warning. She was startled the first time she found him sneaking in. On other nights, she would turn around, frightened to see him standing in her bedroom. She became afraid of what he was capable of. He laughed at her when she changed the locks and added more enforcement to keep him from coming as he pleased. By this time, she had returned the key to his apartment.

Sitting in the limo, she held her clutch bag and looked out the window. The driver pulled over and let her out. She tipped him and walked to the venue with other invitees. It was always beautiful to enter the Plaza Hotel with its bright chandeliers and décor. In the foyer, she signed in and joined the group. This was not an event she wanted to attend, but he insisted, "You are going to go to my event and you are going to do as you are told." She could see him walking towards her.

She did her best to look stoic. She would not look him in the eyes until he finished talking. He ran his hand down her back as he observed her in her new gown.

"Don't disappoint me."

Elegant tuxedoes and ball gowns were surrounded by pretentious snobs. It wasn't like it used to be. She knew she was walking into a fake world. Some of her friends had separated themselves from her and lately, she felt alone. The sommelier came by and offered her a glass of champagne. She took the glass and walked between the crowd. Jen stood out in her golden gown, looking lovely. She could see Jason talking to his usual friends, looking like he was the life of the party. He glanced at her and waved her over. She walked slowly to avoid standing by him.

"What are you doing? I asked you to come stand by me," he whispered. He took hold of her arm and she could feel him squeezing hard.

She whispered back, "I came like you asked me to. Now let me go!"

"Don't start any trouble. This is my night. You don't want to make me angry."

"You're friends are waiting for you," she reminded as she gave half a smile and a gentle laugh. She walked away and stood by a group of people she was more familiar with. Some of their co-workers knew of Jason's aggression. They had always excused his actions with, "That's what makes him a great businessman." It made her sick to hear people rationalize how abuse made someone successful.

The band played music and people began dancing. Jason came over to Jen and asked her to dance.

"Listen, I know you aren't happy with me, but can you just dance with me?"

"Why? So you can look good in front of your friends?"

"We built this business together, so we should be together. Why are you making this so complicated?"

She didn't answer.

He took her hand and slow danced with her. Her face revealed how she felt about his control.

"Can you at least smile?"

"What is with you? Why do you want me to put on the façade and pretend I'm happy all the time? We haven't been happy for a long time and you know it."

"I'm happy because we are successful! Maybe you should listen to me and just follow my lead. I made you who you are. If it wasn't for me, you wouldn't be here. You can't have this without me," he gritted his teeth appearing to smile.

"I tried to make a life for us. I have always had plans to have a future with you. What happened to everything we talked about?" she asked.

"I told you I don't want to be tied down."

"Tied down? This conversation is over."

She broke his hold and walked to the other side of the room to talk to guests. Tony observed the tension and came over to talk to Jason.

"Is Jen alright?"

"Yeah, she's just not in the mood tonight. You know women."

"Hey, I'm sorry, man. Maybe it's time to cut her loose. If you look around, there are a lot of beautiful women here."

Jason watched as Jen proceeded to talk with a gentleman. As she smiled, Jason headed straight for her.

She saw his path and politely excused herself, "Will you excuse me?" She tried to storm away from the crowd.

"I want to talk to you!" Jason blurted out, walking fast to catch her before she leaves.

"I have nothing to say."

"I don't want you talking to any men! We talked about this!"

"You don't control everyone I talk to! Please, leave me alone. I want to stay for another hour and then I'm going home."

"No, we're leaving now!"

He placed his hand around her back and forcefully led her towards the exit. He was making a commotion and guests wondered what was wrong. Jen didn't want anyone to know about their problems. That would put the business in a bad light, so she complied and went with him. He caught a cab and both got inside. When the door closed, Jason began.

"You made me look like a fool!" he screamed.

The cab driver looked at him in the rear view mirror.

"I don't want to have a discussion in a cab. You make no sense when you shout."

"Did you like talking to that man?"

"Yes, I did. He was very interesting and we were having a good time until you swooped in with your jealousy."

She instructed the cab driver to pull over and let her out. She stepped out, grabbed hold of her gown and raised it to walk faster. Jason got out and followed her.

"You know Jen, I could have any woman I wanted, but I chose you. Now you want to change everything and waste my time."

She continued to walk and refused to reply to him. She found her apartment and walked up to unlock the door. She felt Jason close behind her.

"Jason, go find those other women. Go live your dream. Go make it without me."

As she unlocked the door, he forced himself through, shoving and following her.

"What do you think you're doing?! Get out!"

"You think you can end it with me and I don't have anything to say about it?"

"Let me go!"

"Who's to say whether you have been faithful to me or not?"

"You are a piece of garbage! Leave or I'll call the police."

Jason rushed her in the living room and caught her by the wrist.

"You're hurting me!" she shouted.

"Shut up!" At that moment, he struck her in the face with the back of his hand and knocked her to the floor. She was crying while holding her face. As she began to rise from the floor, he struck her again.

"We're done! You're not worth it. You got what you deserved!" He walked out leaving the door open.

She got up, took off her shoes and locked the door. In the mirror her mascara was smeared and her hair was messy. She noticed her eye was reddening and some of the skin was broken. She took a tissue and wiped off her makeup and blood. As she removed her gown to shower, she looked at her distorted face. Jen had never been hit by a man or anyone before. She wasn't sure how to take it or what she should do next. She thought about calling the police but changed her mind because of fear. Opening her closet doors, she stared at her expensive gowns and accessories and took them off their hangers. She began to speak words of disgust and cry talking out what a mistake she made. She put them in plastic bags and took them to the dumpster. From her jewelry box, she admired her first diamond bracelet and took it out to place in her box of letters. She didn't care about the other pieces as much. She could give them back to Jason, but he wouldn't accept them.

The day after the incident, after leaving the café, she noticed an older woman sitting at a park bench. She bought a cup of tea for her and approached her.

"Excuse me, can I sit here?" she asked.

"Of course, my dear."

"I bought you a tea. You look cold."

"Oh, thank you. Do you live around here?"

"Yes. Just a few blocks away. I'm Jen."

"Diane Combs. I love New York. I have lived here my whole life. Now I live with my daughter because I can't afford to live on my own."

"Well, it must be nice to live with family."

"Nothing like it. I used to be a ballet dancer when I was very young. It's amazing how old age changes how our body moves. I can barely get around now.

Anyhow, I went to Julliard because my father insisted I take up dance."

"Really, your father?"

"Oh, yes. Fathers can have a big impact on a young girl's life. He came to all my recitals and would sit in on my practices. When I'd fall down, he would run on stage and pick me up until he knew I could do it on my own."

"That's beautiful. What about your mother?"

"Well, times were hard back then. She just wasn't happy and she left us when I was five."

"I'm so sorry that happened to you. My mother died when I was young."

"And your father? How is your relationship with him?"

"We don't talk."

"Oh, that's sad. What's the reason for that?"

"My mother died from heart disease and he just gave up on being the happy father I knew him to be. He just fell into sadness."

"Being a parent is such a big job. My father tried to do the best he could to make my mother happy. He had those days when he was sad, but he never stopped loving us. It was just me and my brother and we loved him. Dad passed away after I made it big touring with some of the most famous ballet dancers in the world. He got to see me reach my goals and he died feeling like he did a good thing for us."

Jen took the old woman's hand and looked up at her.

"What do you think I should do? I'm still afraid to talk to my father."

"Sweep away any fears you have. You only have one dad and one chance to mend what needs healing. Don't miss your chance."

"Thank you."

"It was very thoughtful of you to care about an old woman like me. Even though it has been hard to just get by sometimes, my happiness is based on those good memories. I was truly loved."

"I have been thinking about making some changes. I feel like I neglected to think about others first, like my father."

"I'm sure he needs you. I wish I had another chance to tell my father what he meant to me. You still have time and I'm sure he will forgive any mistakes you've made."

"I believe you're right about that."

She picked up her backpack and unzipped it as Diane took another sip of her tea. Just then, Jen took out a small box and handed it to Diane.

"I want you to have this. I think you deserve it. It is my gift to you for being a listening ear. I loved hearing your story."

"What is it, dear? I don't need anything for my experiences."

"Please take it. I want you to have them. You helped me see how important loving my dad is. I never stopped loving him or my sister."

"It was nice to have met you. I haven't been feeling myself today and you made me feel better," Diane said. "If you insist, I'll take your gift."

Jen rose and walked back and then turned to look at Diane again.

"I am going to talk to my father, Diane," she called out.

"Good choice. I wish you a lot of happiness."

Diane opened the box and found the jewelry that Jason had given to Jen. Diamond necklaces, a few rings, earrings, and bracelets. Diane was amazed that she had received such an extravagant gift from a stranger.

"My oh my. What a beautiful soul."

Jen came back to her apartment and noticed several messages on her machine. As she played them, she could hear a hang up and no message. They were obviously from Jason. The last message he spoke.

Jen, it's Jason. I'm not sure why you are not answering your phone. I want to talk about last night. There was a misunderstanding I want to clear up. I don't want to lose you and I think we should talk about it. Please call me back.

She pushed the delete button and didn't call back. She wouldn't go back to work until her face cleared up enough to cover the wounds. Jason continued to call. He sounded needy and upset. Jen tried to go about her business, working from home until she felt emotionally safe enough to return to her office. She was taking care of clients and felt comfortable working in her sweats and hoodie. She received a large bouquet of flowers at her door with a note, *I'm sorry.* Jen immediately threw them in the garbage outside.

Three weeks went by until she was ready to return to work. She had Sara, her assistant, lock her office, not letting Jason in. Sara welcomed her back, gave her the spare key, and informed her that Jason was to arrive later in the day. She was nervous about seeing him again. Her style of dress had changed and she had cut her hair. She no longer wanted to be someone she couldn't recognize. She took the picture of her and Jason off her desk and threw it away. She opened the blinds to see the view and let in some light. She got right to returning calls and scheduling meetings. No more parties and champagne. No more limo rides or stuffy dinner meetings, pretending to please people who don't care about her. She wanted life to be simple and go back to who she used to be.

Two hours later, Jason entered his office in his fancy suit to greet his assistant and look through his mail. He glanced up and noticed Jen in her office. He put down the mail and walked into her office without knocking. With the doors made of clear glass, it was easy for Jason to look at Jen while she worked.

"You're back. I missed you," he said.

"I can't say the same about you. Next time, knock when you want to talk to me."

"Can we just put away the sarcasm? Why haven't you answered my calls?"

"I told you weeks ago, I don't want to talk to you anymore. We are business partners and that's where I draw the line."

"I didn't mean to hit you. You just made me angry. You do that sometimes. It won't happen again. Can we just go back to the way things were before we came to New York?"

"No!" she said emphatically.

He walked over and sat on the edge of her desk.

"You know, I can kick you out of this place. You will never work here again. Do you want that?"

"I have already thought about that. You try it and I will sue you. I am a partner and I have a contract. Those clients in my file cabinet are mine. I worked hard to earn their trust. If you stay on your side of the office and leave me alone, we will be just fine. You are scum for what you did to me. Now leave my office. I have a meeting in ten minutes."

"You're going to regret your decision."

"Don't threaten me, Mr. Thomas. Get out!"

Jason left and she felt good standing her ground against such an abusive, controlling snake. She finally saw through all of his lies and had to forgive herself for being foolish enough to believe him. As angry as Jason was, he did not bother her while at the office. He used his assistant to relate any messages to her. It became easier to have him in the same room with her. She just treated him like another employee. She thought it was odd that he stopped pursuing her. Maybe he took the hint to stay away. It was relieving and she no longer thought she should file a police report against him. But it was more important to protect herself from further harm. Not reporting the abuse was just another way to keep fear where it belonged.

One evening, Jen was home watching TV and heard a loud banging on the door. It was locked but she was startled by the sounds coming from the other side. Looking through the peephole, she saw no one. Afraid to open her door, she kept the chain on and opened it a few inches. She saw a white box used for flowers. When she unchained the door and brought the box inside, she found it filled with dead flowers and a card. Its words were created using cut newspaper letters glued in place.

I told you; you would regret leaving me. You are dead to me.

Jen couldn't breathe. She thought she succeeded in getting rid of the man who abused her. It was a cruel, sick, and demented way of scaring her. She put the flowers in a bag and carried them off to the trash. Jason was waiting near the dumpster, watching her, hiding and enjoying her disgusted expression. She could feel the hair stand up on her neck as she ran back inside. She wanted to call the police, but what could they do? Jason was harassing her and getting away with it. Inside, she felt safe. At the office she would not ask for an explanation. She didn't want to give him the pleasure.

Each time Jen went by to the park on her walks, she looked for the older woman again, but didn't find her. Jen showed her caring heart. It was amazing that those who touched her emotionally helped her see that she too was genuine and loving. She refused to worry that she found out about Jason when it was too late.

A few employees quit working for the business and Jason wanted to vet some of the new recruits. Jen was never in charge of his hiring and firing. It just wasn't who she was. A woman came into the building and waited at the desk of the receptionist. She was older, about fifty-five. Dressed in a tweed suit with brown slacks and a scarf around her neck, she felt no need to color her hair. She was tall, very soft spoken, and she carried herself proud. She was quite lovely to look upon.

"Hello, Miss. Can I assist you today?" the receptionist said.

"Yes. I am here to see Jason Thomas. He's my son."

"I will let him know you are here."

She held her handbag and gloves in her hand and looked around at the place her son built.

"Mom, this is a surprise. What are you doing here?"

"I tried to reach you. It's so difficult to keep trying to call when you don't answer."

"Well, hello to you too."

He led her to his office.

"Don't start, Jason. I'm not in the mood for your disrespectful attitude."

"Can I pour you a drink?"

"Ha, you keep alcohol in your office? What have you become?" She was taking off her coat and looking around.

"Okay, why are you really here? France is a long way from here."

"Not that far from New York, Jason. I came here to tell you that your father died in prison last week."

"Well, it would have been better if you would have just left a message about it. What did he die of? Because if he suffered I'd..."

"Jason, stop it! He was sick. He paid for the things he did. There's no reason to rehash his past. I didn't come here just for you to bring up what he did."

"He tried to kill you. There was nothing to like about the guy."

"So, you decided to leave home at fifteen when he was incarcerated. Thank you for leaving me alone with it all."

"Can't you be proud of me for once?"

She looked around, "I can clearly see you made something of yourself. You did this all alone, built this business?"

"Uh, no. I have a partner, Jen Collins. That's her office over there."

"She was your girlfriend, wasn't she?"

"Mother's intuition?"

"No, you just sound disgruntled. She's still your partner in the business?"

"Yes, unfortunately."

"I'd like to meet her."

"No, she probably wouldn't want to meet you."

"I'll take my chances. I'll be back."

Marie Thomas was a counselor and advocate for domestic abuse and helped hundreds of trapped individuals get control of their lives. She knew exactly what her son was like and knew his relationship ended because of how he was.

Marie knocked on Jen's door.

"Come in."

"Hello. Jen Collins?" She reached out to shake her hand.

"Yes. Can I help you?"

"My name is Marie Thomas. Jason is my son."

Jen whispered, "*Oh.*"

"From the look on your face, I can see you were not expecting to meet me."

"Are you here to drill me about why your son and I are not together anymore?"

"No. I wanted to see if you would like to meet someplace where we could talk?" Jen had to think about it for a few seconds.

"Sure. We can meet at my home. I can give you the address. Would you like to come by tonight?"

"I'd like that."

"Mrs. Thomas, is there a reason why you want us to meet?"

"I have a beneficial reason you will appreciate. See you tonight."

Marie went back to her son's office. She wouldn't tell him about her meeting with Jen. He sat at his desk and poured another drink.

"She's nice," Marie said.

"Don't let that pretty face fool you."

"You know what I do. My job is to counsel women and when you talk about them this way, it sickens me. Are you ever going to change?"

"Apparently not. You always said I'd end up like my father. Well, here you go. I think coming all the way over here from France was a mistake. But go ahead, spend your money foolishly. I don't care if your husband died in prison."

"You made yourself clear. I'll see myself out."

Jason wasn't interested in visiting with his mother. He knew her background as an advocate wasn't going to be in his favor. Marie felt sad that he wasn't more welcoming, but she couldn't force the change in him.

That evening, Marie came to Jen's place.

"Would you like some tea or water. I don't drink alcohol."

"Neither do I. I'm fine, thank you."

"May I call you Marie?"

"Yes."

"Marie, why did you come here?" she asked as she sat on the sofa.

"Maybe I should tell you a story first. Jason is my only son. When I met his father, things were great between us. He gave me everything to make me happy. In the beginning, he respected me better than any man I had ever known. We had Jason and he looked happy to father a son. I'm not sure what happened, but everything changed. He drank more, he stopped caring for us, and he became abusive. I loved him, so I kept quiet and told no one what he was doing to me."

Jen looked down at her hands as Marie told her story.

"Did you get help?" Jen asked shyly.

"I did, until it went too far. One night, Jason stayed at a friend's, leaving me alone with a dangerous man. Gerald held me at gunpoint and there was a standoff with police outside our home. I just knew my life was going to end that night. The police finally came in and took him into custody. I was a mess, with bruises all over my body and face. I was so embarrassed to have pictures of my injuries taken at the police station. He went to jail and eventually, to prison. He died last week and I came here to tell Jason. I needed to tell him in person."

"Oh, Marie. I'm sorry that happened to you."

"Now, what's your story? Tell me about you and Jason."

Jen went on to explain how they met and how it was beautiful in the beginning. She mentioned how he lost his temper and apologized to make up for it with gifts. It was no surprise to Marie that the abuse continued to escalate.

"I know my son won't change his ways. He left home at fifteen and got involved with the wrong crowd. He went to juvenile hall and I tried what I could to redeem him. He just headed back into trouble."

"After your son hit me, I was done. He became creepy and harassing. It makes me miss home. My father and I have been estranged for years and this experience makes me want to reconnect with him. I think I want to go back and visit."

"So, you are no longer happy here in New York?"

"I've finally taken back my life. It's hard seeing your son at work every day. He just gives me the cold shoulder and we take care of business. I am willing to work it out for our clients, but he isn't on the same page."

"Jen, I don't want you to end up like me or any of the others I have counseled. Don't let the fear overwhelm you. I am a mandated reporter. If I would have known about this sooner, I would have turned him in."

"I had no way to prove it."

"You were scared. I know it's hard to turn in an abuser. But that just gives them an excuse to hurt someone else."

Marie took Jen's hands and held them. Jen felt guilty for not telling anyone about the night Jason hit her. She was never in that kind of situation before. She put her trust in Marie. With her counseling experience, it was a perfect opportunity to ask her advice.

"Now that the damage is done, what should I do?"

"You have already done what you could to save yourself from harm. I love my son, but you need to make a drastic change for yourself."

"What is that?"

"Why don't I come back tomorrow and we can talk about it? I really like you, Jen. You, like so many girls just get caught up in the romance that hides abuse and control. I can help you. Will you trust me to help you?"

"Yes. I will, Marie. I am so glad you are here."

Marie was only going to be in town for another day before flying back to France. Jen could sleep better that night after talking to Marie. She never had a mother figure to share her adult thoughts with. She was the closest thing to a nurturing mother.

Marie came back to see Jason the next morning.

"Jason, How could you do something like that to this girl?!"

"You're not going to bring this up again, are you?"

"I know you let your temper go too far! You better be thankful I wasn't here when her face was beaten by you! I would have turned you in."

"I didn't beat her. I apologized and let it go and so did she."

"She did not let it go. Sending her dead flowers, harassing her; you're despicable!"

"What else do you want me to say? We're through, so leave it at that!"

"I'm leaving tonight and I really hoped we could connect and fix what went wrong, together."

"What went wrong cannot be fixed. I made my peace with it and I just want to forget about it. That includes what happened with Dad. Can't you see that I am a success without him here?"

"My wish for you is that you find yourself before it's too late. Most of us get better with age. I hope in your case, that is true. Goodbye, son."

After leaving his building, she went shopping in some of the smaller stores filled with handmade lamps and vases. She managed an art gallery west of Paris, so finding places filled with artistic gifts spoke to her. She picked out the perfect gift. She then headed to see Jen.

"I'm glad to see you," Jen welcomed that evening.

"My flight leaves tonight. I'm used to flying late, so I don't mind. I have something for you."

From a brown bag, she pulled out a glass vase and placed it on her table. Jen admired its graceful form and translucent quality. When she rotated it, the blue hues unexpectedly intensified near the edges. It was a fairly large vase, sitting at two and a half feet tall. It loved the light, showing off many hues from the reflection. The shape was also complimenting.

"This is so beautiful. Why did you do this?"

"This glass vase is symbolic. It's so pretty on the outside but empty on the inside. It helps to use this as a way to let you see who you are. Not empty but needing to be filled with love and bring out what is truly beautiful."

Marie used it as a teaching tool to help Jen see her potential and move on from her abuse.

"Now, I want you to tap the vase and listen to the sound."

Jen tapped the side.

"It is obviously made of crystal because of the sound it makes. What do you hear, dear?"

Jen tapped it again.

“I hear a chime, a pleasant ring.”

“Empty, it always makes the same melodious chime. But if you add something positive to it, the sound changes. Filling the vase with beautiful things compliments the look of the glass. You are the glass vase, Jen. You are a very beautiful woman, but you feel hollow inside, staying safe and avoiding pain. Is this true?”

Jen nodded introspectively.

“Now you need to fill the vase with something that is special to you and makes you feel like carrying on. Find what fills your life with hope and inspiration. When I go home, I want you to take out a diary or journal and write down all of the things you always wanted to do or be. Imagine everything you wish. When you are finished, select one as a small step to start your own life.”

Jen was silently crying as she turned the vase. She admired it differently and saw herself as a delicate piece of art that needed to be complete.

Marie passed on additional words of wisdom.

“My dear, please find a way to divest yourself of my son as soon as possible. Sell your share or get out somehow. I wish I could say that business with him will be safe, but I cannot.”

Jen knew Marie’s guidance was accurate. Working with Jason was making her life difficult and her heart really wanted to see the sunlight of what could be.

“What do you suggest I do in the meantime?”

“I want you to think about coming to France with me. Contact me and let me know when you are ready to come. I can help you get your life back. If talking to your father is what you really want, we can make it happen, together."

Jen smiled at the thought of going to France with Marie. What would that be like? What would it feel like to be free of Jason and be reunited with her family? She didn't have to think about whether she wanted to go or not. Her mind was made up.

"I would love to. I will talk to Jason about getting out of the business. I can sell my share and all my belongings."

"You do what you have to. I will send you a plane ticket and we can get your new life started. Don't tell Jason you are coming with me. I will take care of you."

Jen loved hearing those words. All along, this is what she needed to heal her ache. Jen was finally free.

"I wish you could stay longer."

"I have to leave but we will see each other again soon."

Jen wrapped her arms around Marie and held on tight. She could see her new life in her mind and was excited to embark on a new journey, away from Jason. She would listen and get out as soon as possible without fear preventing her.

Marie suggested, "Put the vase where you can see it. Maybe there by the window where the light can expose its full beauty."

Jen pulled a small table near the living room window. She set it on top and opened the curtains a little to frame it. Marie got up and walked to the door.

"There is nothing you can't do. You still have time to let go of everything that hurt you and you will get your life back to where it belongs," Marie counseled as she touched her face. "Take care, my dear."

"I will." Jen felt hope and that meant the world to her.

She remembered a business owner she had contact with a few months earlier. When Jim discovered how good Jen was at her job and built quite a valuable clientele base, he asked her to join his growing group. Things were different in her head at the time and she declined. He was experienced in marketing and owned other businesses with several employees.

Jen called him and laid her proposition out. When he asked why she was selling her share, she didn't provide the full explanation. It was enough to know that she was going in another direction. He was familiar with their company but not with Jason and his business practices. Jen believed him to be business savvy enough to handle any tough situation. He was older and was known to be an excellent manager. So Jen trusted him as a good choice.

It was arranged that Jim would send someone to take over her office in the next two weeks. Everything was set. She prepared an ad to sell a few things. She wrote her sister a letter. She set it aside and didn't mail it. There was so much to do before her flight to France. Jen had plans to take the vase with her as a constant reminder of who she really was and how her giving spirit was just as beautiful. She barely cared about the other things she possessed.

It was all like a dream coming true. Jen was going to be out of Jason's reach and regain her power. She played it over and over in her mind and it made her glad. If she could, she would leave instantly and just forget everything else. Jen was prepared for a huge change. How would Jason take it?

No one was prepared for the actual events that would affect Jen and Jason. The world took a turn as they watched in fear and horror on September 11, 2001.

Chapter 11

9/11

The World Trade Center, often called the Twin Towers, was opened on April 4, 1973. They were numbered as North Tower 1 and South Tower 2 and stood 110 stories tall. At 1,368 ft. and 1,362 ft., they were admired as the tallest buildings in the world and were home to many businesses, like the New York Stock Exchange, Fiduciary Trust Companies, and Xerox Cooperation. The structures attracted 70,000 daily commuters and tourists. From the top, views extended over 45 miles in every direction, far enough to see all five New York City boroughs. Each building weighed 250,000 tons, contained 99 elevators, and 21,800 windows. Every floor was an acre in size. They used enough concrete in the towers to build a five-foot-wide sidewalk from New York City to Washington, D.C.

Nestled in the Financial District of lower Manhattan, the building attracted Jason. He seized the opportunity to move his business to the World Trade Center, happy to grow his success as high as possible. He could have had an office on the lower floor in the North Tower but jumped at the offer of a beautiful view from the 91st floor. It was Jason's dream to be part of the skyline that was loved by many locals and visitors. He worked very hard to get to that point and hoped to share it with Jen for many years to come. He felt that he deserved it all.

But Jason was fooling himself. He believed it was easy to hold on to the woman who fell in love with him. From the time they met, he was good at hiding his true colors until displaying his abusive nature. Uncomfortable, Jen lacked courage to report him until Marie learned the story. She had both the strength and ability to help Jen realize the need to get out fast.

A few days before Jen's exit, Jim came to see the office and meet some of the employees. He was a likeable man and fair to those who worked for him. Jason noticed the man shake Jen's hand and then politely let himself out at 8:25 a.m., September 11.

"Jen, who was that?" Jason demanded.

"That was Jim Coleman. I guess this is a good time to give you the news."

"What news?"

"I sold my share to Jim. He is a good friend and he always wanted to own another good marketing company and we made a deal."

"Why wasn't I consulted? I have a right to know who's coming in this place!"

"He has nothing to do with you. We became separate businesses when you decided to put your hands on me."

Jason was immediately offended. Inside, he was putting all of the pieces together. He had never expected her to sell out. Certainly, Jen had a right to sell her share. He took a breath as it started to sink in.

"Where are you going to go? Who's going to help you pay for your lavish lifestyle?"

"I don't think you need to know any more about what I do with my life."

He narrowed his eyes and tried to figure her out. "This has something to do with my mother, doesn't it? Are you two good friends now? I figured she would have talked you into selling."

"No, Jason. I am taking my life back for myself. I can't work here anymore. You make it miserable. You've hurt me so many times and I am done with you for good."

"You will end up being nothing in your life without me!"

"That's your projection. I would take some time and think about where you are going in life. It's apparent you are on a road to nowhere."

Their conversation lasted a few minutes. She started to the door to let Jason out. He grabbed her arm and jerked her toward her desk. Gripping her other arm he faced her.

He gritted his teeth menacingly, "If I can help it, you are not going anywhere!"

"Let me go!" she struggled.

Jason released and at that moment, there was a loud crash. A deafening boom shook the building. Jen was thrown to the floor and crawled under her desk. Glass lay scattered on the floor and metal was thrown near Jason. His face was bleeding and he coughed violently from fine dust and smoke. He noticed Jen and crawled on the floor in the opposite direction. Jen was trapped under her desk when heavy debris fell on it and crushed it. The ceiling was caved in and destroyed it. Her legs were trapped and possibly crushed underneath and she gasped for air. Her face and hair was covered in dust. She used all her might to push the desk off her legs, but it only shifted slightly. Another thunderous explosion shook the building. Tower 2 was struck as another airplane impacted it. Like an earthquake, they could hear and feel the explosion. It was followed by sounds of people screaming for help in panic and fear. Jason tried to open the door, but it was wedged tight. The air became thicker, making it difficult to breathe. Jen gasped for enough breath to call out, “Jason, Jason, help me!” she screamed straining her voice.

He ignored her pleas, went into a panic, and found himself trapped. Frantic, he searched for an exit. Jason took off his coat and covered his mouth with it.

“Jason, please help me,” Jen continued.

Making no effort to assist, Jason felt his heart pounding from the anxiety and confusion. The window next to him reacted from the pressure above and broke open. With no other way to escape, he stepped to the edge. He impulsively jumped to his death, leaving Jen alone in the rubble and smoke.

“Jason!” She barely got the words out trying to scream as she watched him disappear. The smell of jet fuel made her feel sick. To keep the dust and odor from entering her lungs she removed her sweater and covered her face. Jen’s head began to spin and her body grew tired. She was struggling to breathe and tried to cough to relieve herself. She felt suffocated, like something was cutting off every bit of precious air she needed to live. Her eyes felt a stinging sensation. Some of the dust covered her eyes as she tried to clear away anything to help her see. She lay there helpless and the life was going out of her. A few short breaths and minutes later, Jen Collins stopped breathing and died without anyone to comfort her.

At 10:28 a.m. the building collapsed with Jen’s lifeless body inside along with 16,000 remaining souls. The plane struck floors 93-99. Some felt they had little choice but to take their own life and jump, like Jason did. Many were trapped and died instantly. Those who were able to escape counted themselves as blessed.

Bailee was getting ready for work when she watched the report on the news. Her anxiety was heightened. It was an unbelievable sight. Each time they replayed the airplane footage, it sent a shock through her. She felt helpless knowing her sister worked on the 91st floor. Maybe Jen did not go to work that day. Was she someplace safe? Bailee tried to stay positive and called Jen. Anxiously, she redialed hoping to hear an answer.

"Pick up, Jen, please," she begged.

When she had convinced herself that Jen could still have made it out, she saw the towers begin to fall to their demise. In a plume of smoke and dust, she lost hope. She knew her sister couldn't make it out of that alive. Bailee began to cry. Her chest felt like it was caving in and she wanted to stop breathing. How was she going to help Chap cope with the devastation?

"I have to go to Dad. I need to go to my father," Bailee kept saying to herself as she grabbed her keys. She raced over to Chap's and rushed into the house. He was standing in front of the TV, not moving one inch.

"Dad," Bailee said quietly as she watched her father falling apart.

Chap didn't say a word. He just stood there with tears streaming down his face. Bailee came to him and touched his arm.

"My girl is in there. I need to go get her." He wasn't thinking clearly and mumbled impossible requests to save his daughter. Bailee grabbed hold of his arm to stop him from leaving.

"Dad, we can't do anything for her! Come sit by me."

“No! I need to save my girl.” He struggled to get out of her grip as he cried loud and in fear.

“Oh, Dad. Hold me, please. Just hold me.”

Bailee clung to her father tightly. She tried to get him to hold her, but he wouldn’t move. It wasn’t for several minutes that he turned and grabbed onto her.

“Bailee, it can’t be true. Help me believe this is not true.”

Chap wept his hardest as they held each other. They turned away from the TV, just holding on. Bailee was good at consoling her dad. She helped him to stay calm as he continued to shed silent tears. Bailee suggested they call Lilly with the news.

He began thinking about all they missed out on while separated. He should have made the effort to call more and try to get his daughter back in his life. Regrets surged in and out of his mind, making sadness harder to cope with.

“Dad, we need to make arrangements.”

“I can’t think about that right now. I think I’m going to stay with Brad for a few weeks.”

“Please don’t isolate yourself. Call me or Lilly if you need anything. You know she will help any way she can.”

Chap had no hope of recovering from the shock. Even though Bailee wanted to go to Jen’s apartment in New York, Chap knew it would be too traumatic for him. Planning would take some time since the air was not safe enough to be in the city. Rescuers worked 24 hours a day searching for survivors and the dead. Dust had spread to The Empire State Building. Its plume rose a mile high and drifted another 44 miles. Fine dust and asbestos crept their way into buildings and homes, affecting New Yorker's health. It included particles of concrete, calcium carbonate, gypsum, glass, steel, insulation fibers, and even human hair. City officials initially said there was no risk of asbestos exposure, but that was proven later to be incorrect. The level of carcinogen matter would only dissipate with time and distance.

After giving the news to Nan, Bailee took a few weeks off to gather her thoughts and grieve. Nan's heart was broken for Jen and the thousands of lives who suffered. The whole world was grieving. Even though many hadn't lost loved ones in that senseless crime, countless were traumatized while witnessing the aftereffects.

Marie sat in her living room that afternoon. When she heard the news, it brought her to her knees. Marie lost her son, a son who was troubled and disturbed. When she learned that he took his own life, her ache could be heard for miles. She wanted to scream out the pain of losing the only family she had left. She had hope that he would change and take his mother back into his life. It was obvious he was more than troubled by the terrible things his father had done. She wondered what was going through his mind.

Was Jen alive? She could only hope she was elsewhere. It filled her with sadness that Jen might have missed the opportunity to start a new life in France with her. She was overwhelmed with thoughts of what happened and what could have been. She thought about the glass vase she had gifted Jen. The vision of it was clear in her mind. This was a woman who could see what Jen's life would have been like. Marie wanted to give her everything and it was too late.

After Jen's body was found, her diamond bracelet was still around her wrist. The bracelet was given to Bailee when she received her ashes. The memorial service was held privately with a few family members and friends. Chap sat next to Lilly and her children. He appeared older than he was and his eyes looked tired, possibly from crying.

Bailee prepared a few words about the sister she loved. Chap could do nothing but sit and look upon his daughter as she spoke.

"Welcome everyone. I am so glad you could all be here and celebrate my sister's life. I call it a celebration because she was an amazing woman and friend. Jen was all heart. She was the one who grieved the deepest when our mother died. She was passionate and went for her goals, not caring if anyone judged her. I believe deep inside; she was someone who wanted to be happy. I'd like to think she was happy in New York. None of us want to think about what the last few minutes of her life might have been like. She often thought about us and she loved to care for others. Jen will be missed. My father and I want to thank everyone for the cards and flowers to honor a dear sister, daughter, and friend. Our hearts go out to all the other families who are going through the same pain. We love you, Jen."

When the crowds lifted, they came to comfort Bailee and Chap. Bailee turned to look at the picture of Jen sitting on a table. The flowers surrounding the frame reminded her of their mother. Her love for Jen increased her desire to visit Jen's apartment and learn more about her sister. It still wasn't safe to be in New York because of the recovery the city had undertaken. It would be a few months before she would travel.

A few weeks later, Bailee stopped to see Chap. He was taking the right amount of time off to grieve, but he was still in pain. Brad stayed with him from time to time and listened to him talk out his feelings about missing Jen.

"Dad, I brought you some soup."

"Thank you, but I'm not hungry."

She set the bowl down on the table.

"I think we need to talk."

He spoke softly with grief in his voice. "What is there to talk about? Jen's gone. What else is there to do?"

"Did you talk to the grief counselor like Brad suggested?"

"No. I'm sick of talking about it."

"You know you can tell me anything."

"Did you know Jen called me before 9/11?"

"What? When? Why didn't you tell me?"

"It was two days before the attack. I was so nervous hearing from her. She did most of the talking."

"What did she say?"

Chap clearly remembered their conversation. Recalling how Jen talked about what she wanted and how she missed him, made him smile. He repeated what he remembered.

"Hello, Dad. It's Jen."

"Jen! It's so good to hear from you."

"I'm sorry it took so long to call. I hope you're happy."

"I am now. Hearing your voice makes my whole day. Are you happy?"

Jen paused, briefly thinking about how she wouldn't tell her father about Jason's abuse.

"Yes. I'm happy. I love my job."

"Are you still with Jason?"

"No, we went our separate ways. Dad, I want to see you. I'm making arrangements to leave New York for good and I want to spend time with you and Bailee."

"Oh, you know I'd love that. When do I get to see you again?"

"Soon. I sold my business and I'm finishing up some things. It won't be long. I promise."

"Jen, I never said I love you enough. I should have appreciated how long it took you to grieve over your mother. We were both in the same place and I was wrong to let you out of my heart."

"No, Dad. I was wrong. I remember hearing a conversation you had with Mom saying how you hated your life knowing she was going to die soon. You stopped being a father because of the sadness. I stopped being a daughter because I missed you."

"Jen, if I could do it all over again, I would have never let you go."

"We have a chance to start over. I'm coming home. I love you, Dad."

"Jen, I love you more than you will ever know."

"That was the last thing I said to her. I had waited for years to see her again. I anticipated getting my daughter back. When I saw that building holding my daughter captive, I wanted to die. I missed my only chance to love her all over again."

"Well, you did get one chance to tell her you loved her. I'm so glad you spoke to her. She left us knowing how much you loved her."

"Everyone says life has to go on and that scares me, Bailee."

"I still wonder when the pain will go away. It seems like we've had so much loss. What comes next?"

"I don't know what to do with myself. These thoughts keep crashing into me and I just keep thinking about what she was going through before she died."

"She's not going through it anymore, Dad. She is out of pain."

"You are all I have left. I have this fear that you will leave and life will lose all meaning."

"You know I won't leave you. I wish I knew how to help you get through it. Will you do me a favor? Will you please, get some professional help to make sense of your emotions?"

Chap was listening and knew she was right. The next day, he made a call to a counselor.

Brad was like a brother to Chap. He was there during the bad times when the pain overtook him. It was good to have a friend like a comforting fire, keeping him safe and warm.

Bailee kept her sadness to herself while supporting her father. She would always become optimistic and find a way to deal with her grief. There were times when she privately wept and cried out the pain of losing Jen. At times, she would spill her emotions to Nan, who would listen and add wisdom on how she dealt with her own emotions when life took a turn for the worst.

It seemed like Chap and Bailee found support needed to continue yet more was required to keep their memories alive.

Bailee still awaited the trip to recover her sister's things. She knew of her journal and her love of letter writing. Those were precious and she intended to bring them home. When the time was right, Bailee would go to Jen's apartment and uncover her secrets: to discover why Jen needed to leave New York.

Chapter 12

Carry on the Dream

It had been five months since the 9/11 attacks. After the dust settled, things slowly went back to normal outside of Ground Zero. It would take another three months until workers cleared away the remnants of that day.

The day came and Bailee gathered her courage to peer into her sister's world. What would it be like to be inside her home and see her things? It would be odd without Jen there. Bailee tried to prepare herself.

From the moment she stepped into the airport, she experienced its increased level of security. They were extremely cautious and questioned everything. Travelers were annoyed, but Bailee waited patiently in a long, slow line to get her bags inspected and scanned. The airport seating was packed with people eager to see their families after waiting so long. It would feel good to arrive.

Bailee was not used to the transportation chaos of a larger city. Once out of the airport, she found a taxi and gave him the address. It was located in a nice neighborhood of tightly packed condominiums. It had recently rained and the streets were still wet. Walking up to the door, she put the key in the lock, and turned it. Before opening, she took a deep breath and exhaled. She had waited for this. Inside, it was warmer.

Bailee turned on the light and opened the draperies. Her sister had very little in the way of furnishings. A beautiful sofa, modern coffee table, leather club chair, and a gold lamp, faced a TV in the living room. Bailee silently looked around and ran her fingers across the décor. Near the kitchen, a cork board held pinned pictures of The Statue of Liberty, an Eiffel Tower postcard and photos of her friends. In the center, was one of Jen and Bailee in their teens at the lake. On the wall next to it was a framed letter from their dad. Her kitchen was modern, small, and simple. She loved things clean and easy. Bailee stood where she thought Jen would have. She closed her eyes and pictured what it would be like cooking together with their father sitting nearby. It would have been a precious time together as a family. She could hear Jen's voice and her laughter. It was a welcoming sight to envision.

In her bedroom, she noticed a half-empty closet. It contained warm clothes and a collection of coats and boots for cold New York days. She remembered Jen's fondness for taking walks and meeting people. She was always friendly and curious about different cultures from around the world. She would always smile and say, hello. When they recognized her, she was often rewarded with a hello.

On the nightstand, laid a book. Bailee took off her shoes. Sitting on the edge of the bed, she carefully opened it. It was Jen's journal filled with her private emotions. There were paragraphs about her relationship with Bailee and how she felt lonely missing her family. Bailee went to move her shoes and felt a box under the bed. Inside were all the letters Bailee had sent to her. Her eyes welled up as she looked at each of them. It touched her that Jen counted them precious enough to save.

When Bailee returned to the living room to read the journal, she noticed the glass vase on a small table. It was centered in the window refracting daylight. Outside, the sunlight reached between the clouds to add highlights. From there she could see Central Park. She was amazed at the greens of the park contrasting sharply against the grays of the sidewalks, streets, and buildings. It was an uncommonly beautiful sight, that inspired Bailee to note for a future painting. It was more than she expected to experience.

"Why would she put this right in front of such an incredible view?" she wondered.

Under the vase, was something that looked like a letter or card with the corner showing. Bailee pulled it out and read the back.

"Jen, you are just like this beautiful vase. It can be filled with something to make it even more beautiful. Fill that empty space with life and happier days to come. We will be together soon, Marie."

She turned the card over and noted the address from France. Who was this woman? Maybe the journal would give her a clue. Her eyes wandered until they fell upon an unstamped envelope on the coffee table. It was addressed to Bailee, dated September 10, 2001. Bailee hurried to open it.

Dear Bailee,

I'm sorry I haven't written in a while. I have been going through some changes at work and in my life. I met someone and he turned out to be someone who was not good for me. Yes, it was Jason. I went through a period of sadness and had no way to get out of the misery that was my fault. I have prepared to get my life back and talk to Dad. I'm going to call him, and Bailee, I'm planning on coming home. I can't wait to see and hold you and my father in my arms. I met a very nice woman named Marie. She reminds me of Mom and she has invited me to do something I never thought I could do. I can tell you all about it when I get there. I want to see your reaction when I give you the news.

There are times when I feel lonely and I want to leave this place so quickly. So much has happened and I wish I had the courage to tell you everything that brought me to this point. I've made my peace with all the pain I went through and caused. Marie showed me that my true potential is out there and I'm going to make a new life for myself. I have always wanted to go to France and I may get my chance one day soon. I have so much to share with you. We will be seeing each other soon! I'm counting the days until I can be with you. Give Dad a hug for me. I love you, Bailee.

Jen

Bailee held the letter to her chest. Tears flowed as she heard Jen's words. Bailee missed out on getting to know her sister all over again and restore what they lost. A dark secret had hung between them and all of the clues led to a miserable situation. In the middle of it was a vase and this woman, Marie. It was obviously significant and must have been a part of Jen's newly found happiness.

Taking the journal in her hands, she sat on the sofa and opened the first page. They were words of a frightened woman fearing for her life. The description of her relationship was toxic and was clearly being abused by Jason. She wrote of bruises on her body and face and her fear of involving the police. Jen had no place to feel secure. Words about Marie, painted her as a saving grace for her tumultuous life with Jason.

Bailee had never imagined her sister in an abusive relationship. Jen purposefully avoided the topic in their conversations and letters. Why would she keep it a secret from her sister but tell Marie? Jen was obviously trapped and afraid to tell her family. Somehow, this woman had a solution to help Jen get her life back. And why France? Bailee wanted to find out more about Jen's story from the woman. She recalled Nan learning about herself while in France. Bailee wondered if she went there, could she learn more? It was obvious she put a lot of trust in Marie. Bailee didn't know how they met or what kind of an influence she had on Jen. It must have been powerful.

Bailee would spend that night in the apartment. Sleeping in Jen's bed was comforting, yet sad. As she wrapped the covers around her body, she had to weep. It was going to be a difficult night for Bailee. Thoughts of France and Marie and Jen kept filling her mind, but it was her time to rest. Alone in the apartment felt cold without her sister and reading these words, she felt strengthened.

Bailee got up the next morning and watched the busy streets just outside the window. Tucking the journal and letters in her bag, she decided it would be a safe idea to mail the vase to her home address. On the next block was a package and mail store that wrapped it carefully.

She took the afternoon flight home. With memories of Ground Zero and the victims, it made it hard to stay any longer. She had no idea when the city would fully recover from its losses. Sadness was still in the air and she could feel increased tension in the terminal.

When she landed, her father came to pick her up.

"Hi, Dad. It's good to be back home."

"How are you feeling?"

"I just couldn't be there much longer. There is still a cloud of hurt among the people there. Jen lived a modest life in New York. I brought home some of her keepsakes. One thing I did notice was this glass vase. She had it on a table right in the center of her window."

"What about it?"

"Well, there was a card from a woman in France. I also found Jen's last letter she was going to send me. Oh, and she framed your letter. I thought you'd like to have it."

"I would. Thank you. What did you learn about Jen before her death?"

"She didn't say it to me, but her journal showed that she was very unhappy. She was going through some bad things. I'm not sure where she met this woman, but she gave her some advice or comfort and obviously knew what she was dealing with."

"Where is the vase?"

"I had it shipped to my place."

Chap thought about how difficult it must have been for his daughter in New York. He expected her to see what Jen adored and how successful she was. But to hear that she was unhappy made him feel like he should have listened to Jen more when she was alive.

"I can't stop thinking about the fact that she was so sad. What could have happened to her?"

Bailee wanted to spare her father the heartache about details of her abuse. It didn't feel like the time to talk about it.

"Dad, we can talk about it later. I'm ready to get home."

Chap held the framed letter. He knew Bailee would reveal more when she was ready. Soon enough, he would get answers about Jen.

Bailee returned and could see Nan through the glass gallery doors.

"Oh, let me help you, dear," Nan said as she rushed to open them.

"Thank you. I'm glad to be home."

"How was it?"

"It was difficult to be in the apartment without her, but I embraced every part of her home. The city seems so grim."

"Well, it's still in recovery mode."

"Oh, I'm expecting a package. Let me know when it gets here. It may take a few days."

"Okay. Bailee, if you need to talk, I'm here."

"Thank you, Nan. I may have to take you up on that."

Bailee went up to her studio and unpacked. As she emptied her suitcase, she examined Jen's small crystal jewelry box. Bailee hadn't known her sister to love jewelry. It was obvious she treasured the diamond bracelet she had on when she died. There was still so much to learn about what she went through. While in her apartment, Bailee noticed how much Jen's clothing and style had changed. Bailee remembered her wearing ripped jeans and colorful crop tops as a way of expressing herself as a teen. Their dad hated it and realized she needed more attention than she was getting. In New York, her style was a compilation of elegance and casual; a mixture of outfits for a cozy day walking around Central Park.

Bailee thought more about visiting Marie. She might be able to crack the mystery behind Jen's words in her journal. She looked at the postcard again and put it on her nightstand. There was still an ache in her heart for the woman who didn't deserve to write about so much sorrow. Maybe there was more to Jen than that. Bailee doubted that she knew her sister as well as she thought. She wondered what happened to Jason and what compelled Jen to want to come home. Her thoughts wouldn't rest until she made the trip to France and talked to Marie.

Nan was sitting at the front desk looking over her agenda for the week. Bailee came down to talk to her.

"All unpacked?" Nan removed her bejeweled glasses.

"Yes. It feels wrong to do anything without feeling sad about Jen."

"Sadness is only a small part of being human. We are capable of so many different emotions."

She pointed to an oil painting across the way.

"You see that work right there? When he started it he was depressed. I know that. He told me. But if you look closer, you will find some very interesting colors making up his shadows. He found other emotions that led him in the right direction."

"I never noticed that."

"A small smile can make a big difference in a person's life. I know you feel sad about losing Jen, but don't you think there are so many things that you love that can also make you happy?"

"I'm grateful for my dad. You know, after my mom died, he lost a lot of weight. Before he sold our house, he wanted to help Brad with the landscaping. I think it was a way to deal with all that went on."

"Everyone has their way."

"Sometimes, I just have to scratch out a heavy charcoal landscape to get me through it."

"Me, I liked the French countryside."

"Nan, what brought you to San Marino?"

"Oh, that's a long story."

"I have time."

Nan wasn't prepared to tell Bailee about what made her leave France. She had to pause to gain her thoughts. Bailee sat across from her. Nan adjusted her bracelet and raised her eyes.

"I met a man in France. He wasn't French. He was Italian and English. He was a gifted painter and I noticed him at several art shows but he never spoke to me. One day, we were assigned to sit at the same table at a banquet. I was a little older then and he was so handsome and quiet. Suddenly, he started asking me questions about myself. It was after my second marriage ended. We seemed to have so much in common. We started a beautiful friendship that led to love. He was going to be the one."

"Going to be? What happened? Where is he? Why aren't you with him?"

"I don't really know where he is. We had such a wonderful time together and then one day I turned around," her eyes changed expression. "And he was gone. He never said he wanted out of our relationship or that he met someone else, he just left me alone."

"And San Marino?"

"I have had my share of heartaches in life, but that one was hard to get over. I had a friend here who wanted me to get a gallery started for her. She wanted me to stay with her for six months and market her art and learn the business. I thought it would be a good thing to get away from France to repair my wounded heart. I never planned on staying, but here I am. When I offered to buy the gallery from her, she started another business on the East Coast."

"When was the last time you went back to France?"

"It's been years. Each time I think about going, I remember Giuseppe and what he left behind."

"Have you ever tried to find him?"

"No. I'm sure he moved on with his life. I just assumed I should do the same."

Bailee showed Nan the postcard.

"I found this at Jen's place."

"This is from Normandy, near Veules-les-Roses. You remember me telling you I lived near there? Who did Jen know from Normandy?"

"A woman named Marie."

Bailee related the story about Jen, the glass vase, and the friendship she developed with the woman.

"I'm thinking about finding her. There is so much more about Jen I need to know," Bailee contemplated.

"Are you thinking about going?"

"I think I have to."

"You still need closure. This woman may have some answers you need to mend that broken heart of yours."

"I know you're right. There is so much to learn. I can't wait for you to see her vase when it arrives."

"Now I'm curious about that."

"I don't know if it's valuable but it's beautiful."

She reached for her hand. Both women loved sharing stories about love and loss. Nan always believed that love healed all wounds. Despite all she had been through, she still held a beautiful outlook on life. Bailee needed that. Nan was just the person to step in.

Nan began to tell about the history and beauty of northwestern France. Bailee pictured its loveliness, wanting to be there. She would save a few paychecks to make the trip. That would give her time to research where she was going.

Bailee's hope was that Marie could unlock more about Jen's need for love. How did this woman manage to help heal her pain? What did Jen tolerate from Jason? What kind of a woman was Marie? Soon enough, Bailee would get to know who saved her sister from emotional harm. She too, might need Marie.

Chapter 13

For Jen

After patiently waiting, Jen's vase was delivered to the gallery. She carefully examined it for any damage while admiring its translucent blues. She found a special place to display it near her kitchenette window. It was as if it belonged near the light. Nan found it equally interesting as a piece of art. Both remained curious why the woman related it to Jen.

During the following week, Nan shared some of her favorite spots to visit, like Les Andelys in Normandy. The green hills and gorgeous views inspired her as it did many artists. She described homes near the water's edge and the rock formations topping off and complimenting the trees surrounding the countryside.

"You have to try the white Muscadet wines from Loire, they take your breath away. Let's see, Normandy is known for its "four C's" in cuisine."

She looked up trying to think.

"Camembert cheese, cider, cream. That's three, and calvados. That's apple brandy. Oh yes, creperies and galette cafes are omnipresent. You will fall in love with them." Nan embellished.

Nan made the area sound warm and inviting. Bailee could feel the romance of the region, imagining the comforts of France. It would be the trip Bailee would never forget, her first time out of the country. She said she was doing this for Jen. Inside, she admitted it might be equally important for herself. If only she could have taken this trip with her sister. Bailee asked Nan to join her, but her history with the place still held too much sadness. Bailee hoped she would take the leap and join her another time.

Bailee researched the area and learned about the French Riviera, the cathedrals of Notre Dame, as well as The Louvre. They also reminded her that exploring it first-hand would make it come to life in a more vibrant way. She planned on taking her trip in the springtime. Some of the villages went into hibernation after summer and there was not much to do in Normandy until spring. To see more of the country, she planned on renting a car with the freedom to see it all.

Soon after Bailee returned from New York City, some of her paintings had sold. A gallery owner on the coast admired Bailee's talent and bought eight pieces. He wanted to commission her for another ten if she could add some ocean to the background. His favorites were her floral landscapes. She gravitated toward portraying foreground flowers with pinks and pastels her mother adored. Bailee loved to bring joy to buyers, and at the same time hated to part with her art.

Going to Normandy would be like watching her canvas coming to life. In her journal, Jen anticipated her trip to France and enjoying its beauty. Jen never seemed like the kind of girl to love such things. It was wonderful to see how much like her mother she was. Jen's sadness being kept inside, had not allowed her to be herself. Bailee could sometimes read the signs, but always felt on the outside. There was always a deep compassion and no judgement for her bad decisions. Now that her sister was gone, Bailee knew it was time to find out more about what Jen loved.

Chap decided to visit Bailee at work. He rarely took the time to drive over.

"Hi, Dad."

"The place looks nice."

"Nan is very generous and kind for letting me live here."

"Uh, Bay. I wanted to talk to you about going to France."

"Don't you want me to go?"

"I know you want to go but going so far away, well it just makes me anxious. After all the terrorism and you going half-way around the world, I..."

"I think it will be fine. It's safer to travel now. Nan has been to Normandy and she knows the area very well. I have been educated on what's in store."

He sighed a small relief, "Is she going with you?"

"No. She is not able to make the trip. Dad, I'll be okay."

"You want to find out more about what was in that journal. What if you find nothing?"

"That's why I'm going. I want to go and meet this woman who helped her be free from whatever it was that was hurting her."

As Bailee climbed the stairs to her studio, she related what she found under the vase. She handed her father the glass vase as they tried to guess what Marie meant. She mentioned the vase to her father before and now they wanted to know more about the meaning.

Chap always knew his daughters were beautiful. He looked up at Bailee who was every bit as lovely as her mother. Deep inside, Jen was also like Caryn.

When he heard from Jen last, she sounded different. As she spoke, Chap closed his eyes and listened. She talked about her dream to regain their relationship and how she wanted to treasure more time with him and Bailee. She exposed the special place in her heart for her mother and how she could not let go of her anger. It was painful how Caryn suffered and died undeservedly. Jen needed more time with her and that became possible. She had fantasized that her mother would miraculously be healed and they would continue their life together without fear. Jen had such dreams and her anger kept her from revealing her true feelings. She talked about drawing with Bailee, those times when her father played with them and camped out in the backyard. She remembered the days she begged to hear stories he knew as a kid. She lamented how it all vanished when he focused on losing Caryn. She tried asking for attention and special times together and he regretted putting her off. She felt ignored and unloved. As Chap listened to those words, tears streamed down his face. He didn't want Jen to hear him cry. It was enough to listen to her voice. He had not realized how badly she needed him and it opened his eyes to the truth. He wished he could make up for what he did not do and felt the weight of his mistakes by ignoring Jen's needs. He wouldn't make the same mistake with Bailee. It was a breakthrough for Chap, who wanted to make things better while keeping the memory of his wife and daughter alive. Bailee reminded him that he was a loving, caring, and good father. Even if things were not the way he wanted, he was still someone Bailee looked up to. She wanted him to let go of the guilt and trust her as a grown woman.

When Bailee finished explaining about the vase, Chap smiled, imagining Jen's appreciation for the gift. Having never met Marie, he was grateful for everything she must have done. Her future became bright and promising. She reiterated what the trip meant to her. With Bailee holding his hand, he understood that she must go.

"Bailee, I think I am scared because we lost your sister to terrorism. I don't want it to happen to you too. It frightens me to be without you."

"What are you going to do while I'm gone?" Bailee asked.

"I'll go to my counselor regularly. Brad always checks in. I'm learning how to cope. Don't worry, I'll be fine."

"You are my hero, Dad. I'm so proud of you and I think Mom and Jen would have been proud too. We will be alright."

Chap could embrace the moment. The confidence in himself and in his daughter were strengthened. He was speaking to a grown woman who was still crawling out of the pain of losing someone so precious. He would never let go of their childhood; memories branded in his mind along with the playful times they enjoyed. If he listened closely, he could hear the laughter of his two girls. There was something about that conversation that made Chap realize his daughter was mature.

Bailee was going to France and relive what Jen would have wanted. She would imagine her right next to her, taking it all in. Bailee was going to embark on the trip of her life.

Chapter 14

Take the Walk with Me

Bailee was nervous traveling alone to a new place. She didn't know exactly what to expect when she landed in Paris. The weather was not like Southern California. There were more clouds and it was a bit cooler. A light jacket would do just fine. Approaching the desk where her rental was reserved, she waited in line. She had a written list of all the special places Nan recommended. She had watched television programs about the country and most of all, Paris, with The Louvre, Eiffel Tower, historical areas, and common places for tourists. Traveling around the arrondissements of the city was something she only dreamed of. What she was going after had deeper meaning. Nan encouraged her to enjoy herself, focus on clearing her head and make memories. Being there was dedicated to Jen. It took some getting used to, driving through the city. It looked as though no rules applied and numerous cyclists flowed with the traffic. She drove near Champ de Mars, 5 Av. Anatole France, the address of the Eiffel Tower. It was so lovely to look at and more romantic in person. She wondered if she would have time to reach the top and suddenly, she felt lonely. She wanted someone to share the moment with her. Bailee felt amorous feelings flow through her. She had always heard people call it the city of romance. Seeing it first hand, she came to believe it.

After a good night's rest in her hotel, she went to get a coffee and take a morning walk. Bailee was used to walking and it looked like perfect weather to search out places to relax and let the city infuse her. She noticed a quaint patisserie close by her hotel and a few more on the other side of the street. Right around the corner sat Café Henri. She loved the outdoor seating full of customers busy with conversation. Behind the window, an array of pastries and croissants were displayed. Bailee smelled the coffee as she entered the café and waited patiently in line. Listening to the patrons order their favorite drink in French was interesting. She wasn't sure if the barista spoke English but she would give it a try.

"Excuse me. Do you speak English?" she politely asked.

"Yes, not very well. What can I get you?"

She ordered a croissant and black coffee with room to add cream and sugar. Since the seating was crowded indoors, she squeezed between diners outside and reached a small vacant table. The overhead fabric awning swayed gently in the breeze. She put down her coffee and prepared to sweeten it. The gentleman across from her watched her pour in sugar and cream and heard the spoon against the mug as she briskly stirred its ingredients together. Before she could enjoy what she put together, he felt impelled to interrupt.

"You will have to excuse me. Why do you think you have to put that in your coffee? You don't think our coffee in Paris is good on its own?" he inquired.

"Um, is this any of your concern?"

"I consider it an insult to adulterate good coffee. It says, "This coffee is bad until I poison it."

"I'm not poisoning my drink. I really think you need to just keep your thoughts to yourself." As she lifted her cup, he chimed in again.

"I'm happy to see you are complimenting your concoction with a croissant."

"I don't want to hear criticism from some stranger at another table who doesn't know how to mind his own business. I'm going to ignore you."

"Ah yes, then I will come to you."

By that time, Bailee was quite annoyed. Because there was no other place to sit, she determined to put up with it.

"My name is Lucas Henri."

"Do you expect me to introduce myself?" She avoided looking at him. A view of the street activity was better for her.

"I've known a few Americans and I don't recall any of them being this rude," he smiled.

"I'm sorry. I'm not trying to be rude. No one has ever judged my coffee drinking before. It's a little hard to take."

"Well, I am a lover of coffee. Did you know that Voltaire drank over forty cups a day? Balzac beat him by fifty."

She turned to look his way. "So, you're a connoisseur on coffee and how to prepare it?"

"You could say that."

She took a bite of her pastry as he watched.

"Do you enjoy that?"

"You ask a lot of questions. If you think this is not making me uncomfortable watching me eat, you are wrong."

"I'm asking about how your palate is enjoying it because I made that lovely pastry."

"What do you mean, you made it?"

"This is my place. Café Henri. I make delicious treats people around the world enjoy, like yourself."

"You don't look like a pastry chef."

"Well, I'm young but I have been around food most of my life. My grandfather taught me everything about baking and how to make it perfectly."

"And your coffee education? Where did you learn that?"

"Experimentation. I just prefer a good black coffee. We make the best here."

He was sincere.

She looked at her cup and asked, "So, you want me to try it without anything added to it?"

"Yes and it will be on the house, as you Americans say."

Bailee liked listening to Lucas. Maybe she enjoyed his accent which displayed his passion for good food. He continued to express his love of working with special flour and butter to fluff the pastry just right. His passion was putting his energy into baking perfection. It was to praise and honor his late grandfather who raised him. She noticed he liked to talk a lot. She could barely get in a word.

"I need to get back into my kitchen, but may I ask why are you visiting our city?"

"Well, I'm here to see someone. A woman who lives in Normandy. It's personal."

"If you'd like, I can show you around. I was born here and I can teach you about Paris."

"That's okay. Thank you, though. I have a friend who used to live here and she gave me the skinny on some of the places to see."

"Oh, you're right. The best way to see it all is to search for it without the help of a true Parisian."

Bailee thought about it for a minute. It would be nice to have a tour from someone who knew all about the city. She was going to pass on that one. She felt confident enough on her own.

"Excuse me. Don't leave yet," he requested as he went inside.

Bailee had no clue what his intention was. There was a stranger wanting to help her on her visit but it felt too awkward to accept an invitation from someone she didn't know. He seemed well-known by his customers and the place was packed with people who loved his coffee. Even though he offered, she was going to see the sights on her own. Lucas returned as she took another sip.

"Here, I brought you another coffee. Trust me, you will like this one. You know, no one should see Paris alone."

"I'm seeing it alone because I don't know you."

"You think I am some kind of criminal? I could be the map to your roadway."

"It's nice of you to offer but, no."

"Well, you missed your chance. Now, taste the coffee."

Bailee made a face and sipped her coffee slowly. She had never liked black coffee before.

"How is it?" he asked.

"Surprisingly good. Thank you. Now, may I finish my croissant?"

He nodded with a huge smile. As she sat there next to the busy street, her eyes caught the shadows playing between archaic buildings. As cyclists rode by and cars stopped and started, they seemed to flash off and on between sunlight and shade.

Lucas was still standing close by. "What time do you get up?"

Surprised, she replied, "I don't have a time to get up. I am hoping to sleep in. You know, the time difference."

"You should get up early. It's good for you. I'm up every day at three."

"How nice for you," she sighed.

"I'm glad you like the coffee. Will you come back tomorrow?"

"I'm not sure. I do like the place."

"Then why the uncertainty? Come early and we can talk a little more about Paris."

"I'll think about it."

He seemed to be a very jovial young man, kind enough to help her see the sights. It would definitely help her along the way. As he went back into the kitchen, he turned and asked her,

"What is your name?"

"Bailee. Bailee Collins."

"It was nice to meet you, Bailee. *Au revoir.*"

As he waved goodbye, she was curious about this man who was very kind and friendly to her and the regulars that were enjoying his creations.

Bailee took it upon herself to explore the historical district. Filled with centuries of culture, some places held a sadder part of history. Visitors were everywhere. She wasn't used to being in such a popular place alone and the world felt too big for her. Along the narrower streets, cooler air passed through. The experience gave her new reasons to be glad she came even if it wasn't shared with a friend. She stopped in at a small shop and chose several postcards of where she wanted to go. A small statue of the Eiffel Tower held her interest. She thought about Lucas' offer and could see why he wanted to take her on a tour.

That evening, Bailee ordered her dinner through room service. She had unpacked her things and placed the journal and postcard from Marie beside her bed. Combing through her wet hair after a well-deserved shower, she wondered what she would say to Marie when she found her. It felt awkward making a surprise visit from California to see a perfect stranger. She avoided rehearsing. Bailee couldn't see how it should be uncomfortable for either of them. But she still wanted to think about what she might say or ask from the stranger who knew her sister. When she got up to look at herself in the mirror, she recalled a private moment with Jen when their father was sleeping. They were still teenagers.

"Jen, are you scared sometimes?"

"I guess I am. Why?"

"Well, when you fight with Dad and scream at him, I get sad. It scares me when you get angry."

"You wouldn't understand."

"I want to. Why are you angry?"

"I think about all the things we could have done with Mom if she wasn't so sick. I had so many dreams and hoped she would heal and we could be a family again."

"But we are a family."

"No. Dad is so separated from us."

"Really? You don't think he loves us?"

"I don't know."

"Sure you do. How would you feel if you lost your soulmate, someone you loved since you were six? I think he misses her more than we know."

"What about us? Don't tell him this, but I miss him so much. I need him as much as Mom did."

"Jen, try, just try to talk to Dad with love. Think about how it makes me feel when you cry."

"Bay, you are my best friend. You always seem to have it together. I wish I was more like you."

"I am not as together as you might think. I have bad days when I think Mom will be in the kitchen making chocolate chip pancakes for us on Sunday. I cry too."

"I know. I just hate asking for love."

"It's easy. Just say, I need to be loved, Dad. See, just like that."

"Oh, Bailee. I love you. I can try."

"Really try."

They hugged afterwards and it appeared that Jen felt better.

The next day Jen had moved out. Bailee was completely surprised. She wished she could see into her sister's world more clearly. Marie must have seen the pain she was going through. Jen's need for love was quite concealed. Bailee had watched her sister close herself off from others over the years. Inside, she was still delicate but refused to let it show. Recalling their earlier tender moments helped Bailee realize Jen's desire to reveal that side of herself. Obviously, Marie was able to sense it and help her see the need to speak to her father and return home. Bailee was grateful for putting her sister on the right path and imagined what life would have been like had she survived. Now it was Bailee's time to walk where her sister would have gone, to be where she wanted to be.

She put her head to pillow early, trying not to think about the meeting with Marie. The time change told her body it was time to rest. When morning came, Bailee was ready for a walk to the Eiffel Tower. It was early and shops were still opening up. As she walked her way around the streets, she thought of her sister. Bailee was there, in a city full of people, walking alone. It took longer than she planned, but as she approached that marvelous structure, gazing at its beauty, it became very real. Her favorite admiration was seeing it in person.

Tourists were taking pictures and sharing hugs together. In the background, she could hear a man strumming a guitar, adding romantic ambience. As wonderful as it was, it also felt sad to see it alone. Her mind placed Lucas beside her. It was kind of him to offer his company and make the trip more meaningful. However, Bailee didn't take well to strangers, especially in a foreign country. She sat on a bench and watched people go by. A family with two young girls caught her attention. The parents were taking pictures of them laughing together.

They held hands and danced. Bailee especially noticed their mother smiling at their playtime. She missed her own mother who used her limited energy to play with her girls. With the loss of both Jen and Caryn, the joy of being there just wasn't as pleasurable as she thought it should have been. Then she reminded herself how important it was to go on making her life happy. But she was still missing out on something.

"You will never find happiness by wallowing in sorrow," she told herself.

She got up and put on a smile as she looked around. Her eyes caught heavily shadowed trees behind the lawns. People were passing by in brightly colored clothing and it reminded her of an impressionistic painting. She took a photo of it for later. They seemed to all have someone. The truth was, she didn't really have a friend there. At least one person had made the effort to be friendly. She had someone to talk to at the café and he was interested in showing her around. She resolved to appreciate what she had at that moment. As she strolled around the tower, she imagined Jen walking beside her.

"Did you think we would ever get the chance to be here?"

"No. We always worried about Dad and making him happy. He wanted us to come without him."

"I know. But I wish he were here. This is our time for an adventure. We have to see it all!"

"I wouldn't know where to begin."

"Who cares? Let's share each day together and see where the wind takes us."

"Jen, have you lost your mind?"

"What? Bay, we're in Paris! Take it all in and take the walk with me. Get a little crazy. There is no better place to be than here with my favorite sister."

Bailee opened her eyes. She loved using her imagination when she thought of what could have been. If Jen was there, she would want to see anything and everything until late in the night. Jen brought out the fun in Bailee and it would have been the best time of their lives if she were there. She thought about seeing Lucas at his café. Instead, she decided that a trip west suited her better. It was time to find Marie and learn more about what could have been...with Jen.

Chapter 15

Hold My Hand

The scenery through Normandy held Bailee in awe. She followed the Seine as it coursed its way to the sea. On the northern bank was Le Havre and the southern side of the estuary was her destination, Honfleur, where the inhabitants call themselves Honfleurais.

She could see the port's blue waters reflecting its idle boats. Aged houses with slate frontages looked just like the art by Claude Monet and Eugene Boudin. Bailee could see why Marie chose to live there. The old world buildings and cottages made her feel like there was no other place to be. She was suddenly excited and nervous to meet the lady behind the mystery. Marie was the only one who drew close to Jen. To Bailee, that was a big deal.

She reviewed the address on the postcard and checked the map one last time. She finally located her street and made her way to the long driveway. At its end, a small cottage sat surrounded by green pastures. Romance seemed to fill every detail surrounding her. Marie's home was quaint and cozy to look upon. Carnations and snapdragons bordered the front of the home and oak trees shaded its right side. Woven rattan chairs and a small table nested beneath. Guests were beckoned from the driveway by a pathway lined with multi-colored bricks that led to a bright yellow door. It was more than Bailee imagined. It was peaceful. She felt held by the beauty. Walking up to the door, next to a copper bell, she noticed a brass plaque, *Maison de la Paix*, House of Peace. She took a breath and rang the bell.

Marie came to the door, "Hello, can I help you?"

"I'm here to speak to Marie Thomas."

"I'm sorry, I'm not accepting any new patients at this time." Marie began closing the door when Bailee spoke up.

"That's not why I'm here. My name is Bailee Collins. Jen was my sister."

Marie put her hand over her mouth, shocked. A familiar pain returned as she looked at Bailee.

"How did you find me?" Marie asked.

"I went to Jen's apartment and found this postcard. She kept a journal and wrote down some kind words about you. The postcard was underneath a glass vase near the window. Were they from you?"

"Please, come in."

As Bailee stepped inside, she could smell Jasmine tea and fresh-baked biscuits. Pictures of friends and family hung on the wall near the fireplace. The décor was just as she pictured a French cottage to be. A curio cabinet housed antique China. Scandinavian platters, bowls, tea cups, and saucers were also on display. On a lace doily, fresh flowers centered on a small dining table. A stack of mail was placed next to it.

"I love your home," Bailee complemented.

"Thank you. I have some hot tea. Would you like a cup?"

"Yes, thank you."

"Please, have a seat in here." She pointed to a floral sofa. "You sure came a long way just to see me. Since I haven't heard from Jen, I assume she was a victim of the 9/11 attacks."

"Yes. She died in Tower 1. The loss was hard to take. I wasn't sure why I came here at first."

Marie looked at Bailee for a moment and said, "You came here because of Jen."

"I wanted to honor her and take her place and I think that is why I wanted to see you. You had a good influence on her. When I couldn't reach out to her when she fell apart, you held her up and helped her live again," Bailee explained.

"Jen and I had a special friendship. Because she was with my son, I knew I had to step in and help her gain control back. You do know her history with him."

"Oh, yes. You are Jason's mother. I understand why you were involved. Why did she need control back?"

"Jason was aggressive and he took it out on Jen. She was in a trapped situation and without her crying out for help, I could see where her life was going. I had my difficulties reaching out to Jason. I miss my son every day."

Marie set the cups on the table nearby.

"Where is he now?"

"He died on 9/11. He committed suicide before his building fell."

"I'm so sorry. I didn't know. When I read her journal, she mentioned that she felt like a prison cell would have been better than being with Jason. She mentioned a few things about abuse."

"It may have been too hard to face the fact that she was a victim. I have been there myself and even though I wanted to get out of it, I couldn't bring myself to let go."

Bailee dropped her head, thinking about the abuse and mistreatment. She was never brought up around that kind of misery and it must have devastated Jen with every breath she took in. Marie came closer and took her hand.

"Bailee, don't be too sad. Before the collapse, she was safe. It was important to save her from further danger from Jason. I don't want to think about what else he could have done to her."

"Marie, you asked her to come and stay with you. She wanted to come here to France. She had made arrangements."

"She wanted to start a new life. Jason made a good life for himself financially, but physically and emotionally, he was dangerous. When my son learned she was leaving, it set him off. Somehow, I believed I could use my professional skills to help him get better and change. After a while, I just stopped trying."

"Thank you for not giving up on Jen. I was so happy when she said she wanted to come home. I guess you could say, I want to live the life she would have wanted."

Marie nodded, "I completely understand."

Bailee lifted her eyes to the window. She wanted the mood to change because she loved this place. "How long have you lived here?" she asked.

"Shortly after my son left home, about twelve years ago. Did Jen ever talk to her father?"

"She did. She had plans to leave New York and the next day, 9/11 happened. It was hard to believe she didn't get the chance to come home."

"She was on the right path. I have seen many women and men suffer through abuse. Some had their lives taken from them, others made it out alive. I'm so sorry Jen lost her opportunity to make it here."

Bailee nodded, "How are you dealing with your loss?"

"When I watched the news, I feared the worst. I felt like I was never going to be the same after I lost him. I know he was troubled most of his life."

Marie continued to explain the struggles that plagued her as a mother, how her energy was expended helping him avoid trouble. Early on, she decided to become a counselor and help others trapped in their own sadness. Marie could see that Jen was someone who wanted to regain her life after ending her relationship with Jason. She grieved for a long time after discovering his suicide. With no other family, her old wounds felt exposed. She had hoped that Jen was somehow still alive and back with her family. Now with the news of her death, Marie relived her loss.

She spent years assisting victims of abuse, helping them regain their life and many succeeded because of her patient demeanor. When Marie suffered her own feelings of pain and isolated herself, she hid from her own pain by shutting out friends. Time helped her come out of that dark place.

"After my ex-husband went to jail, I sold the house and went searching for myself. Jason left home while still a teenager and we stopped communicating, so I traveled a bit. I went to India and a few other countries looking to start a new life. I found that I loved art, even though I am not really artistic. I saw a lot of beautiful pieces, original art, vases, and carvings. France was the last place I visited and I made this place my home."

"And the vase?"

"The vase reminded me of someone who had a passionate soul. Like you, Jen was a beautiful woman. But she felt empty and lost. I wanted her to remember who she really was and fill her life with everything she wished for. Her smile came back and she was ready for a new adventure. The vase is lovely on the outside, but it has a deeper meaning when it is filled. It's always better with beautiful flowers or anything that makes her happy."

"I found some notes in the vase. They were reminders that she can have hope to be happy again. Positive affirmations, I guess."

"It's good to know she was on her way to being where she wanted to be. That's another good reason not to be sad anymore." Marie took another sip of tea.

"I took the vase to my home. When I look at it, I see Jen. I think our conversation is opening up a new opportunity for me."

Bailee opened Jen's journal and shared it with Marie. Inside were pictures of Bailee and her family. There were many good times in their close unit. Marie noticed a picture of Caryn.

"I have something I would like to show you. I have a local art gallery and I'd like to take you there, if you have time," announced Marie.

"I would love that! What a coincidence. I work at a gallery too."

On the way to the gallery, Bailee absorbed the breathtaking scenery.

"I want to see everything. I love it here."

"It's a different life but if you're ready for it, it can be an exciting way to live."

Marie had a good feeling about Bailee's presence. It was as if Jen was sitting next to her. The unexpected visit came at the right time for Marie. Both women helped each other move on and regain what made life joyful. They passed the charming hamlets of Veules-les-Roses, the prettiest and oldest spots in Normandy. Thatched cottages and stone houses bordered the tiny Veules River.

Marie noted, "Not to sound like a tour guide, but this looks just like the villages of Venice. It has been here since the 4th century."

An old water mill still turned with splashing sounds dropping rhythmically. She looked at Bailee. With the window down, her hair was blowing in the wind. Marie stopped the car and Bailee got out and ran over to the bed of flowers near the river. Surrounded by nature's canvas and art, Bailee bent over and closed her eyes as she took in the fragrant aroma. It smelled so sweet. She then stretched her arms out and let the wind touch her. This made Marie very happy. Bailee was letting go of that familiar pain and Marie could see true hope ahead for the two of them.

Arriving in front of the gallery, Bailee could see the building was old. It had a charm her gallery would never match. Marie turned on the lights and Bailee looked around at the different styles that artists created.

"What do you think?" Marie asked.

"It's lovely. There is so much expression here."

"Sometimes we get art that is a little understated and unusual and they do sell."

"I know about unusual art," Bailee said.

Bailee was struck by a large painting on the opposite wall. She stared at it and slowly walked toward it.

"This is my mother."

"Jen gave me her picture. Because it was her favorite, I had an artist put it on canvas. So many people have wanted to buy it, but I just can't let it go. I don't think I will ever sell it."

"My father took this picture. She didn't always feel beautiful because she was sick. It's like she is here with us."

The artist portrayed Caryn with her long auburn hair and standing in a garden of vines. She was wearing her favorite white dress. Chap wanted that image in his mind forever. It was one of the times Caryn felt lovely.

"This is what I wanted to show you. I was waiting to surprise Jen with it. Since then, it has complemented the gallery and is admired by many visitors. Bailee, you have so much to be happy about. Despite tragedies, you have a wonderful life. These women in your life have given you a good start and because of them, you will get the life you have always wanted."

"I would have never believed it until now."

Bailee talked about how she started at a young age using her artistic expression to take her out of the world she grew up in, creating her own beautiful places. Bailee stepped to the side to catch a different lighting. It felt like she was in that garden with her mother. She remembered being in her mother's arms, holding Jen's hand as their mother stroked their faces with tender fingers. Bailee walked over to a large mirror in the corner and looked at herself. She took down her hair and turned her body as in the portrait and whispered, "I love you, Mother." She could see her. It really was a special place to be. She could take Jen and Caryn anywhere with her. The love Caryn showed to her family helped Bailee see that she was also a gifted woman who knew how to love.

Alongside Marie, she could see a beautiful, real world. Everything around her was an inspiration for painting new pieces of art. The flowers, villages, and bodies of water, lifted her to new heights of appreciating beauty.

Marie took Bailee to a small café near the gallery for some lunch and Madeleine cookies. The sounds of the harbor carried across the sea breezes. Locals and visitors walked to and from its attractions.

"Have you had a chance to get to know any of the local people yet?"

"I did meet this pastry chef at Café Henri. He's not a fan of cream and sugar in coffee."

"Café Henri. I've been there. Lucas Laurent makes the best desserts. I have to agree with the coffee issue. It should stand good on its own."

"He said his name was Lucas Henri."

"That is his name. Lucas Henri Laurent. Henri was his papa's name. He named the café after him. Henri was a famous chef in many parts of France. His father traveled all around France and cooked for a lot of communities. His favorite place was Toulouse. I think he liked the history."

"Why didn't he tell me that?"

"Maybe you held back because he was a stranger and you were new to Paris. He probably sensed you were uncomfortable speaking to a man you never met. What do you think?"

"You're right."

"You liked him, yes?"

"No. He was nice but annoying at the same time."

"Don't underestimate the French. They have a romance we will never understand. Have you gone back to see him?"

"No. Should I?"

"Well, being friendly is different from being romantic. If I know Lucas, I think he may have wanted to be your friend."

Bailee was guilty. She was rude to Lucas. He was likable by customers who knew him and his grandpa. She was easing into French life and developed second thoughts. She should give it another chance and start over.

"I hope I didn't come off unkind."

"I don't think you were unkind. Everyone knows the history and facts about Henri. I think you will find a good friend in Lucas."

"Being here is changing something inside me. I think I want to belong here someday."

"You may get your wish. Go deep into a place that shows you where you belong. Gather it together and embrace what your heart tells you."

When they returned to Marie's cottage, they took a walk, waving at her neighbors tending their garden. Marie spoke some French and greeted them with a hug and a kind word. She introduced Bailee and they returned a warm smile and welcome. Marie invited Bailee to spend the night. She expected the trip to be a negative space. So far, she was the happiest she had ever been.

The morning sun rose over the fields, leaving them with dew and Bailee prepared to go back. She couldn't stop thinking about Lucas and how she owed him a proper apology. After a light breakfast, Marie offered an invitation.

"Bailee, you are welcomed back anytime. If you get the chance, bring Lucas. It will be good to see him again. It has been a while."

"Thank you Marie, for taking me to a different place."

The two embraced and Marie gave her a squeeze to show her appreciation and newfound friendship.

As Bailee drove away, she could see Marie waving until she turned out of sight. On her way back to Paris, she kept recalling the little things Marie had expressed. Even Lucas was seen in a different light. She liked his company. Keeping that to herself, she wasn't looking for a love affair. Marie told her that Lucas may need a friend and that was what she wanted to be. She realized that she left something special at Café Henri, the opportunity to be a good friend to someone who may have thought she was worth it. Bailee didn't want to miss what could have been.

Chapter 16

Welcome To My World

The tourist season was in bloom and Café Henri was at its busiest. Bailee took her time dressing for the occasion and weather. She felt her best walking and admiring the streets of Paris and felt at home as she expressed, 'Bonjour,' to passersby. She didn't care if they were locals or visitors. There was a new sense of happiness since her visit with Marie, who provided history about Henri and Lucas. It was obvious that they were well-known and his patrons felt like family. Marie gave Bailee a lot to think about. The young man had more history with people and the food industry than she realized. She prejudged him and that was not typically her way. When arriving in Paris, her primary mission was getting answers about Jen. But, she had come to love France, creating lasting memories and visions to paint later. She often browsed her pocket translator. Loving the sound of the language, she wanted to fit in among those who made this place home. She was on her way to see Lucas and hopefully give a peace offering from their first meet.

Closer to the entrance of the café, Bailee could see servers in short, black aprons cleaning tables and presenting orders. The smell of fresh brewed coffee quickly brought back memories of when she was here last time. She couldn't wait to recapture it with her first sip of the day. Standing in line, she caught sight of Lucas in his white apron, greeting a family by the window. Unknowingly, a smile crossed her face and she shouted out his name.

"Lucas!"

He looked around to find her waving and made his way through the crowd, eager to see her.

"Bonjour, Bailee. You came back. I was losing hope you would ever return."

"I missed this place."

"Oh, you need a coffee. It is chilly today. Please, let me get you a large cup."

"No sugar or cream."

"Parfait! I knew you would grow to love it."

He went behind the counter for a coffee and poured one for himself.

"Come, let's take a seat over here," he pointed.

"You didn't have to do that. I could have waited in line."

"*Non,* I am happy to see you. Today, you are my special guest."

She wrapped her fingers around the warm cup and took a sip. A young server interrupted with a plate of assorted pastries to enjoy while they talked. Her eyes glanced around others enjoying the same. She took in the sound of their conversations. As she turned back, she found Lucas looking directly at her.

"So, what brought you here today?" he asked.

"Well, I want to apologize because I was rude to you. I don't want you to think all Americans are unkind."

"I accept your apology. I just think you are uneducated about me and what I am doing here. My mission is to serve these people."

She felt the need to start as if she was meeting him for the first time.

"Can we start over? I'm Bailee Collins."

"*Enchante, Bailee.* Lucas Henri Laurent," as he put his hand out.

"I went to see my friend in Normandy. She told me she knew you and your papa."

"Oh? Her name is?" he urged.

"Marie Thomas. She said you are an amazing chef. Your grandfather left a legacy and many people loved his cooking."

"Oui, he was the best. This is why I want to keep his dream alive."

"I would like to know more about you and what France means to you."

"I have never known any other city to call home. There were so many places my grandfather wanted to take me. He loved the history of France and learned everything he cooked from his father. I miss him every day."

"I understand what it means to miss someone you love. When I went to see Marie, I learned about my sister and the trials she went through in her adult life. She wanted so much out of life and she missed our mother very much. I miss them both."

"At first when Henri passed, I just wanted to give up. He left me his home and everything that was his. Walking in his footsteps just wasn't the best for me. I could never match up to what he accomplished. Then I found a cookbook he had written. It had never been published. When I opened it, I found recipes that were faded and difficult to read. As I cried tears for him, I turned the pages to find that he had dedicated it to me. He loved me very much. It was like he was talking to me and asking me to go on without him. So, I used some of the money he left me to open the café."

"I can see how everyone loves it here. You should be so proud."

"There was a time when I wasn't proud. I could never be as good as he was. I would only see my failures in my future."

"You are so jovial around people. I could never imagine you feeling down about yourself."

"I had to find where the passion was and take what he left behind and hold it dear to my heart."

Thinking about his grandfather made him melancholy. He wanted to elevate his feeling and offer something to Bailee.

"Would you like for me to cook for you? You can come to my home and we can talk where it's a little warmer."

"I think I would enjoy that," she smiled.

Bailee had reinforced his confidence. She remembered hearing that Lucas could use a good friend.

"You have such a great history. Marie said she would like to see you again. Maybe some memories will come back to you when she met your grandfather."

"They are great memoirs."

"I think you get your passion for food from Henri. Never let go of that," Bailee reassured.

"Merci, Bailee. I have to be here for a few more hours. After that, we can walk and I can show you part of my city."

"I found it lonely seeing the sights without someone to talk to. I am looking forward to it."

He stared into her face and she did the same. Catching themselves looking at each other, they both laughed. Lucas stood up and went back to work and Bailee decided to do some shopping along the street.

When Lucas went to the back of the kitchen, he could hear the noise of dishes being stacked. His friend noticed him talking to Bailee.

"Is she an *Americain*?" Jean inquired.

"Who?"

"The girl you were talking to."

"*Oui.* She just wanted to get some coffee."

"I saw her here a time before. She's beautiful. I think you like her." Jean dried another plate.

"She is a nice girl who needs a friend. I'm going to show Bailee around later."

"What about Monique?"

"What about her?"

"She has been asking for you."

"That's been over for a while now. I can't believe you brought her up."

"She seems to think you still love her."

"We both want other things in life. She ended it first. I can never go back with her."

"Lucas, I know your grandfather's death left sadness in your heart. I just don't want you to get hurt again if you like this Bailee. She will be going back home and then where will you be?"

"I don't think you need to worry about me."

"*Mon ami*, I care about you."

"I know. I think this girl just needs a friend. That's all. I can be the friend she can trust."

Jean knew that Lucas had been through a lot in his life. He wanted him to continue on a journey of loving life and living happiness. He remembered carrying Lucas through some of the worst times of his life.

Lucas had shown Bailee only the parts that were joyful and wasn't sure what he was feeling for her. He wanted to keep his emotions from getting carried away. For the time, he enjoyed her company and wanted to see her smile again. He saw something in her the last time that wasn't there on their first meeting. He could never forget sitting across from her that day. Bailee seemed to be happier. He wanted to know where that came from and wanted her trust.

Lucas hadn't seen Monique in several months since their falling out. When Jean mentioned her, it brought back a fear that she would return and try to make amends. At first, he tried giving her another chance. She broke his heart once again and the risk felt more about desperation than love. He and Monique were together for three years. She was there when his grandfather died. Jean and Monique were his only support at the time. During the worst of his pain, she avoided him and then ended it. He had planned to marry her and love her forever, but the devastation was too much. She had come to the café last month to talk, but he couldn't get the words out about how much she hurt him. He began to question whether he was really in love with her.

Bailee had suddenly and almost accidentally come into his life and he felt a change come over him. Her own losses were a common ground made to support each other. Monique had been his only experience with love. His parents had not been in love. His father left right after he was born and his mother left when he was six. Lucas was abandoned to his grandfather.

Henri was an older man and wasn't quite sure how to care for a grandchild who may have been traumatized by abandonment. All he knew how to do was love him and care for his immediate needs. He stood him on a stool at his side whenever he cooked, teaching him about spices and ingredients that make food so desirable. Lucas quickly learned to respect sharp knives and flames. Nights by the fire, he would hold him in his arms and read to him until he fell asleep, some days in French and others in English. As he became older, Lucas did most of the reading. Every day was the same routine and it always involved cooking. Henri refused to leave him with anyone and took him everywhere. Paying a baby sitter felt selfish to Henri. Many times, the train ride home left Lucas exhausted. He never said much as long as he was in the arms of his papa. As he watched his grandson grow into a man, he was proud to see him endure. He learned much from Lucas too. Patience came easily for the elderly man who loved cooking and baking pastries. Henri believed that butter was the key ingredient for enjoying life when it came to food. He could put butter in anything and it always tasted better. *Beurre* was life to Henri and that's what Lucas carried with him, even after he passed away. He became the epitome of Henri.

Bailee arrived early to meet Lucas. It was just about lunchtime and the sun finally came out to warm their day together.

"Are you ready to see Paris through my eyes?"

"You're the guide, take me where you want."

Lucas hadn't felt that happy in a long time. He could read what was in her mind before even asking. He guessed accurately where she wanted to go.

"I know you want to see the Eiffel Tower with someone. Let's go."

He began to tell her the history of the beautiful attraction millions of tourists admired over the years. He painted a picture of what Paris and all of France meant to him.

"If you come to see it alone, it becomes a time for reflection, maybe finding love. Take in its beauty, it takes hold of you and you are no longer alone."

"I never thought of it that way. I was undecided about coming at first because I couldn't share it with someone I loved."

"You were obviously close with her."

"Jen. Here is a picture of her."

"She is very pretty, like you."

"Our mother was so lovely. My father said I looked like her."

"You are close with your family?"

"I just have my dad now. Mom passed away when I was young and then my sister died on 9/11."

"You said you came here to see Marie. Did you find what you were looking for when you talked her?"

"I got more than I wanted. She opened my eyes to see things from a larger perspective. I think Marie helped me fall in love with France. My sister was going to live here. I wanted to live through her and see what she was missing. It would have been beautiful if she would have had that chance."

Lucas allowed silence between them as they gazed on the tower. Then he began to speak.

"How do you feel now that you are here with me? Are you no longer lonely?"

"I'm better now. Thank you for being here with me."

"I too, am glad you are here with me."

"Where did you learn English? You speak it very well."

"We had to learn it in school. It was required and it was hard for me. Henri also knew some of it. Now I am glad I can speak English because I can talk to you."

"I like the French better. It sounds more romantic."

As they walked, Bailee learned more about local culture. Lucas even gave her some lessons on speaking French. When she didn't get the accent right, he found it comical, but did not laugh at her. Each place he talked about inspired another recipe. He talked about dishes he learned like Coq au Vin, Cassoulet, and Gougeres, a dainty cream puff. Pear tarts and Palmiers were embellished with a romantic description. Quiche Lorraine and Potatoes Dauphinoise were two of Henri's favorites which won him praise and honor. Lucas decided from an early age that he would not stop learning until his dishes tasted like a master chef's. He experimented to make it better and to his success, diners loved it. Crowds of people flocked to enjoy what Henri taught his grandson to master with dedication and hard work. Bailee could see it when he spoke about his drive to make Henri proud.

She looked at him and grinned, "You love to talk about food."

"Food doesn't just fuel the body; it gives pleasure and pleasure is happiness. Henri said to savor every bite, never take it for granted. It is to be enjoyed. It is life."

"I have enjoyed some good food in my day. You know what they say about the calories."

"What calories? Who thinks about that? It is the hard work that brings a smile to the face who gets to taste the finished product."

"So, what are you going to cook for me?"

"Ahh, you will have to be surprised. Come on. We will take the train to my place."

As they boarded, Bailee observed individuals who traveled to and from work every day. Some lived far away and worked inside Paris.

"You come to work this way every day?" she asked.

"Oui. I am used to being on trains. I can't imagine any other way. Are you comfortable?"

"Yes. I haven't had the chance to ride a train since being here."

"You will love it."

Bailee looked out the window and watched tall buildings and tight housing turn into cottages surrounded by fields. Valleys with green pastures, stone fences and small farms warmed her heart. When they stopped, they had another two mile walk to get to Lucas' home. Bailee was experiencing what Lucas did each day. She was not used to it. The road was hard-packed rock without a sidewalk. Sometimes a car would pass and they would wave.

"How could you do this every day?"

"I never think about that. Henri and I took many trips together and even in his old age, he didn't mind. If you enjoy your surroundings, you don't think about it."

"Okay, you win. We'll keep walking."

He described homes that stood unchanged for centuries and families who had bent over backwards to help their neighbors. The air began to chill. Just before nightfall, Bailee saw a tiny cottage nested against a group of trees. Lucas pushed the door open and placed wood in the fireplace to warm his home. Her eyes roved the room to find his bed in the living area. It was as small as a studio apartment back home.

"You were raised here?"

"Papa only had room for himself. When I came here, I was six. He built me a small bed next to his. He made this place a safe home for the two of us."

He lit the fire and grabbed a blanket for Bailee. He placed it on her shoulders.

"Thank you. It's cold inside."

"It will be warm soon. I will make us some tea."

"How do you shop for your food?" she asked.

"There is a little market not too far from here. I ride my bike or take the train. I make sure to stock enough so I don't run low. Most of the time, I just eat what's left from the café. I make it work."

"Have you thought about moving closer to work?"

"No. This home is part of my family. I could never sell it just to be comfortable."

"That's what makes you unique."

"Everyone has their reasons for the things they do. What makes you unique?"

"Uh, well, I paint. I am an artist."

"An artist. You would fit in very well with the Parisian community. Art is part of life here."

"I don't feel like I'm that good of an artist."

"No. Don't say that. Anything that shows the part of who you really are, is unique. It belongs to no other but you."

"That's true."

Bailee was finally getting warm and she could see the food he was preparing. She unwrapped the blanket and looked at the table of ingredients. She could see rosemary, shallots, white truffle oil, and some greens. He was making a dish with a Lyonnaise salad. Watching him put the scattered ingredients together was fascinating. He was quietly humming and occasionally sung a French line as he chopped and diced. He mixed the dough and put it together with precision. His hands moved quickly with the experience of a master. His movements showed his love for it.

"Are you sure I can't help?"

"You are my guest. It is my pleasure to do this for you."

She took her tea and sat in the only comfortable chair near the fireplace.

"It smells wonderful. It's cozy here."

"I had to learn to live alone. After Papa died, I took walks, wrote recipes and mingled them with Henri's. I would get up very early and go off to the café to make everyone happy. That place has become my family and my life."

"After my sister died, I put so much of myself into my artwork. I had never realized how lonely she was. Marie said she had an emptiness that was like a beautiful vase."

"How do you mean?"

"She needed to be filled with something beautiful like love. A vase is only a vase when it isn't filled with flowers. Jen began to feel beautiful again and it was because of how Marie cared for her."

"It was a good thing to have her there when she was needed."

"Jen is my beautiful vase."

He crossed over and sat on his bed.

"I'm sorry I never got to meet her. I'm sure she would have enjoyed France."

Bailee nodded.

"So, what's your story? What do you know about your parents?" she inquired with curiosity.

"Henri never told me much about them. His daughter was my mother. Her name was Suzette. From what I know, she fell in love with someone my papa didn't like. They fought about it and she ran off to marry him."

"What was his name?"

"I don't know. Henri never told me. He didn't want his name mentioned in his house, so I never heard it."

"Did Henri ever see his daughter again?"

"No. She held my hand when we walked up to this house. When he opened the door, she bent down and told me that this was my home and not to cry. I did cry when she walked away. Henri called out to her, *"Suzette, Suzette. retour, fille."* He took me in his arms and wiped my tears, cleaned me up and fed me. I had never eaten so much and then I fell asleep by the fire."

Lucas held back tears brought on by the memory.

"He taught me how to love and endure any trial that came my way. Before he died, he asked me not to feel sad for him. He lived a good life and I should use everything he taught me to make it on my own."

"And it was hard for you?"

"Very hard. I would hear his words in my mind and I would push myself to listen and do what he thought was best."

Bailee didn't know what else to say. Lucas had gained strength to continue to live on. She was feeling everything he said about his life and felt fortunate to have a father. Bailee had Chap, just like Lucas had Henri. Her gaze met his and the firelight reflected in their eyes.

"What are you thinking, Lucas?"

"How similar our stories are. The day my mother left me, I thought I would die from sadness. Henri gave all he had and more to make sure I was happy. Your father did the same for you?"

"He tried to. He went through depression after my mom died. They knew each other since they were six. He had never known another except her. I gave him what he needed to continue to live. He encouraged me to make this trip."

"Didn't he want to come?"

"No. He was right. I needed to be here and deal with it alone. And I am glad I did."

Lucas opened a bottle of wine and Bailee could smell the food nearing completion. He took out a baguette and a large stick of butter and placed it on a wooden board along with some grapes and Brie. In a small jar was a fruited jam from his neighbor.

"There is a family that makes jam every year for me. Our food is almost ready to enjoy. Do you like wine?"

"I love it. I used to go to these events where they served some of the finest wines from Italy and of course, France."

"We are going to have Sauvignon Blanc."

"I'll take it."

Lucas took out the hot dish along with a salad and set the table with mismatched plates with hairline fractures.

"I have beautiful dishware at the café, but I can't seem to part with these," he pointed at the dishes. "Henri did have long-stemmed wine glasses and always said, "Wine should be enjoyed in style. It complements the meal, even a poor man's Ratatouille."

Bailee watched in anticipation as he served her first. Everything that had to do with preparing food gave him happiness. She could smell the bacon, rosemary, and caramelized onions. As he drizzled truffle oil over the top of steaming potatoes, it's aroma grew in intensity.

"What is this called?" she asked quizzically.

"Potato Galette. It's like a rustic tart. One of my specialties."

Bailee took a bite and suddenly her senses rose to new heights. They related what they loved about life and what made it all worthwhile. Bailee was discovering things about herself and could see why Jen wanted to make the country part of her life. Lucas related stories about patrons he knew and some of the funny anecdotes they told. Café Henri was like a hangout place for those who loved Lucas and his delicacies.

She took a piece of bread and put a little butter on it. Lucas observed her ritual.

"Is that all you are going to have?" he asked.

"I don't eat a lot of butter."

"Why not? Give it a try. Then take more and add some jam."

"Okay," she said reluctantly.

She took a bite as he watched.

"It's good," she commented.

"How many dishes have you eaten that have butter in it?" he asked.

"Well, a few."

"Everything taste good when you use butter. Many say butter is bad for you, it can even kill you. Henri would say, "What a way to die," as a joke. Butter makes life feel good. Some say the French use too much of it. We say, *non!* We love to please our palette and make the soul happy; butter is one of those things."

"I have to admit, I have had foods where butter is very important. Where would the croissant be without it?" she mused.

"*Exactement*! That's what I'm talking about. In the short time you will be here, you will become French before you know it."

Bailee turned away to stand closer to the fire. She was thinking about having to leave France to go back home. Lucas hesitated before asking her a question as he watched her mood change.

"Bailee, what is wrong?"

"I love this, being here with you. Even though I miss my father, I don't want to go home."

He walked over to her. In his heart, he didn't want her to leave either. He took her hand into his and spoke softly.

"Bailee, I don't want you to go. This is the happiest I have ever been in my life."

"I didn't expect to feel this way. Maybe we shouldn't talk about this."

"Feel what way? Tell me."

"The way I feel when I'm with you. I feel special."

"You don't have to look away when you say that. I thought about you every day. I waited for you to come back to the café. When you didn't show up, I missed you. I thought I did something that made you stay away."

She wrapped the blanket tighter around herself as she looked into the flames, "No, no, it wasn't you. It's all so new."

"Are you afraid of it?"

"No. It's just that I don't want to think about going home and not seeing you. I found a good friend in you."

"If it's meant to be, it will stay with you. For now, you are here and you have nothing to fear. I am here with you."

She felt it was bold to put her arms around him. But he drew her closer and it was only natural. He held her near the warmth of the fire, tightly reassuring her safety. After the wine had been drunk, it was time to retire for the night.

"We should get some rest. We have to catch an early train back to Paris," Lucas reminded.

He made a place for himself on the floor and gave Bailee the bed. The fire was slowly going out. Lucas laid an extra blanket on her body for warmth. It was quiet except for a spark in the fire and his old clock keeping time. Bailee couldn't sleep.

"Lucas?"

"Yes?"

"Thank you for letting me into your world."

"There is so much more to see. Does your father call you anything else besides Bailee?"

"Yes. He calls me Bay."

"I like that. Goodnight, Bay."

"Goodnight, Lucas."

Bailee knew what she was feeling. She wondered if she was falling in love or did she love his company. The stories he told and how he chose to love life had changed everything for her. She found a new breath and a will to be happy again. Paris brought her to Lucas.

Chapter 17

Henri

Nice was considered one of the most beautiful places near the Italian border, facing the deep blues of the Mediterranean Sea. With views of the French Riviera, many flocked to capture its breathtaking scenery and fall in love with its coastline. Other than the fewer homes and resorts, it was no different in 1920.

In a small, modest apartment, housed a family. Gabriele Laurent and his wife Aurelie Cadieux lived above a flower shop that was a popular spot for visitors including Aurelie. She adored flowers in her home and missed the gardens she grew up with when her mother was alive. Gabriele's father was French and his mother was Italian. There was so much they had in common living near the border. Gabriele was a romantic, loving the tradition of food and family. Even though he missed his Italian roots, he loved to make his wife happy living the French lifestyle. She was expecting their first child. With a new baby arriving soon, the anticipation was exciting and he took pride in caring for her. Gabriele was self-taught and started off baking desserts for his neighbors and cooking outside his home. Eventually, he sold his food on the street and then opened a small restaurant near his home. Gabriele loved mixing the Italian flare into his dishes. While he was busy in the kitchen, Aurelie toured the shops and galleries, admiring the local talent in colorful paintings, etchings, and statuaries. After receiving an inheritance from her mother's estate, they decided to risk a move to Nice. It was an elite city that cost more to live in. Gabriele did everything he could to make his wife happy because it was where her heart wanted to be.

The day came when Aurelie gave birth to their son in their small home. They named him Henri Benoit Laurent, after Henri Matisse. The French artist was praised for his colorful and fluid draftsmanship; the sculptor who specialized in painting. His collections were in the Musee Matisse close by.

Aurelie spoke to her child in her native language, but her husband used Italian and French. Giving their child a start in the French world was a dream for them. Henri grew to be a happy child in a household of love and food. He remembered his father singing Italian songs at night, and during the day his mother sang in French. Henri often accompanied his father to watch him cook. He would sit on the counter or a stool for him to look on.

He wanted to do what his father was doing, eager to get his hand into the dough and mimic what his mentor was creating. Henri would receive a small ball of dough and practice forming it. It put a smile on his father's face. Gabriele would reveal each secret recipe and ingredient put into his dishes with a passion for its power. At the age of four, Henri was helping prepare delicate desserts and learned the culinary art of fine cooking. During his teen years, he read cookbooks and occasionally read stories about the history of France. Using his sense of touch and smell, he explored the finer elements to compliment foods his father prepared. It became his first love and that led him to work alongside his father. Henri knew no other life outside of the restaurant. Observing the patrons smiles and laughter while tasting, felt like a gathering of family. After all, that was how he was raised. The dust of flour on his clothes, the smell of garlic in the air, rosemary, and thyme resting alongside his olive oils and truffles was his love, until he met Amie.

Amie was a young girl, about seventeen. Henri was much older, twenty-four. She was very fluent in French and other languages. She was beautiful, whimsical, and well-educated for her young age. She was well-versed in the country's history and wanted to plant roots when she finished school.

Amie grew to love the restaurant and when she didn't see Henri, she would leave to return another day. Henri was too busy to notice her fondness of him. She visited more regularly and eventually asked him to join her for a chat over coffee. He admired how she carried herself for a teenage girl. She was quite mature. When his father noticed, he warned about being distracted by her beauty. The more Henri spoke with Amie, the more he enjoyed her company. Late night walks and sharing sunsets together along the beach brought them closer and they married a year later. Amie gave birth to a daughter, Suzette. With complications during the birth, sadly Amie died as Suzette was born. In one night, Henri lost the love of his life. He lost focus on his love for food and became overwhelmed raising a child on his own. Henri's mother aided in giving his daughter the love and care she needed to grow up happy. That love helped Henri find his strength and love in the art of cooking once again. When Gabriele tried to teach his granddaughter how to cook, she was not interested. Henri could sense his daughter missing the love of a mother. She needed a complete family and there was always something missing in her life. When she neared adulthood, she left home.

Henri lost his mother that same year and his father was slowing down and working fewer hours. Henri was carrying most of the weight of the restaurant and encouraged his father to retire. Still missing his wife, Gabriele decided to retire and turn the business over to his son. That summer, Gabriele died in his sleep. Henri knew it was a difficult time, but he had to carry on his father's legacy of good food. He tried to get in touch with his daughter, Suzette, but she never called or wrote. As the years passed, Henri put everything into his recipes. It became an obsession, an obsession that gave him the pleasure he needed to move on from the losses he was experiencing. Soon, many would come and enjoy the creations he prepared to bring people together. His father taught him all about his Italian heritage since he was young. He loved their passion and love of family and passed it on. He wanted his world to be full of life and laughter. He would greet everyone entering with open arms and seat them at their favorite table.

"*Bonjour, mes amies!"* Where is the rest of your family?" he exclaimed loudly. Everyone looked forward to his welcome. It was a kitchen where love was prepared. Using his parents estate funds, he purchased a small cottage in the country, a train ride from Paris. He still missed his daughter and tried many times to find her. It had been seven years. She finally came to his home to see him. As he looked out the window, he was graciously surprised to see her face.

"*Bonjour, Papa."* There was no excitement in her tone. She may have been feeling guilty for avoiding her father.

"*Cherie*, after all these years, you have come back to me," he replied with elation.

He invited her into his home to prepare a meal for her. He could not contain his happiness.

"Please, let me cook for you and you can tell me where you have been."

"I can't stay, Papa. I wanted to tell you I am married."

"Married? Well, where is this man who stole my daughter's heart? This is a celebration!"

"He could not make the trip. I am going to have a baby next year."

"This is good news. But you don't seem happy. Why is this?"

"He left me and I am going to raise my child alone."

"How could a man leave his wife? Did he love you?" Henri wasn't used to that kind of family dynamic. He could see his daughter was hurt at the thought of being alone.

"He did love me but he doesn't want a child."

Henri felt his emotions flow, thinking about his grandchild being without a father. He never wanted to know the name of the man who made his daughter cry. He would never hear his name the rest of his years on earth.

"You can stay with me, *mon petit* and I will help you raise your child."

Suzette thought it was a good plan and she did stay with her father for a short time. After the birth of her son, Suzette moved out and searched for her son's father. Henri named his grandson Lucas Henri. He didn't want him to have his father's last name, so he gave him his own. After Suzette left her father's home, she settled in a small place outside of the city, living with a family she had grown up around. They kindly took her in and when Lucas was six, his father came back into Suzette's life with the condition that she would give her son away. She was still in love but did not want to give her son to strangers. He was convincing and Suzette let her emotions take over and decided to give her son to Henri. The boy never knew his father, was never held or even acknowledged by him. Suzette had loved her husband more than her son. To Lucas' surprise, he never seen either of his parents again.

When his mother dropped him off before going to her husband, she was alone. His father chose not to be there. Suzette had tears streaming down her face as her son watched his saddened mother. She stopped the car and Lucas asked his lonely question. *Ou sommes-nous, mere*? Where are we, Mother?

She couldn't answer him until they went to the front door. Henri was in his early fifties by that time and lived alone most of his life. He was caught by surprise when he saw his daughter and grandson.

"Suzette, come in," he invited.

"No, Papa," she said curtly.

She bent down to face her son and explained, "This is going to be your new home. He will take care of you and you will grow up happy."

After that, she closed her eyes, turned, and walked briskly to her car. There was no goodbye nor did she look back. Henri called out, but she didn't respond. The hand that held her son's for the last time was placed on her own cheek as she left.

Lucas couldn't understand why he was there. Everything seemed like a blur, full of confusion. He didn't remember Henri and assumed his mother would return soon to get him.

Henri's head dropped, feeling the shock of a mother abandoning her child. He knew she would not return. He also realized that in his old age, he was going to have to play the difficult role of father. Henri never really understood her reasoning. He assumed she was with a new man or Lucas' father. Whatever the reason, it was a happy and a sad day for Henri and Lucas. Suzette was never seen again.

Henri treated Lucas as if he was his own child. He came to the conclusion that since he couldn't reach his daughter in her younger years, there was a new opportunity to be a loving father again. Although he didn't know how to raise a child, he could use the skills his father taught him and the nurturing love his mother displayed to help him along the way. Putting Lucas to bed, he looked upon pictures of his family history with sadness, photos of his parents and his love, Amie, the birth of his daughter and the funeral of her mother. The highs and lows of life showed age on his face. His love for family and food never stopped him from being happy to be alive. He soon fell in love with Lucas, who was always by his side. Like his father, Henri taught the art of preparing delicacies and fine food. When shopping, Henri would pinch off a bit of the greens and taste the freshness, educating Lucas about the seasons and the right time to pick fruits and vegetables.

"Smell is crucial and taste makes the eyes shine," Henri would say.

They would enjoy wines together, take walks where his parents once lived and learn the history of Nice.

It had been Henri's dream to travel with his father to different cities and teach culinary skills to newcomers. He never got the chance and then his father became too weak to travel. After his father's death, he did go to Giverny, made famous by Monet's paintings. He loved its settings because they reminded him of his mother. As a lover of fine art, she instilled its appreciation in him. Henri's next destination was Toulouse. His wife, Amie, often talked about its history and always wanted to live there someday because of her love for the ancient city. Memories were flooding for this elderly man and the weight of the world sat on his shoulders.

He would raise Lucas without fearing he would leave him or stop loving his craft. They grew close in that little house. Lucas learned a little Italian and asked to hear stories of his family. Throughout the years, Lucas grafted into being like his grandfather. Taking train rides into Paris, he would also greet those who knew Gabriele and Aurelie. Henri showed Lucas how he could become great at cooking, just like his ancestors. Henri avoided talking about Lucas' mother. When older, he told the story about how he came to live with Henri. He tried not to paint a bad motive on his mother. It did not faze Lucas. He was always happy to call him Papa. Although Henri made a great deal of money in his day, he never considered living in the heart of the city. His calmness came from a place of solace and that was the countryside.

Butter was an essential part of the kitchen and was always on the table during mealtime. Handling dough and turning a few ingredients into a rich meal warmed Lucas' heart. He enjoyed cooking for his grandfather when his aged hands could no longer knead or whisk whipped cream and Chantilly. Days arrived when Henri moved less and his tired body rested more. He tried not to look back longingly at those times spent baking and feeding hungry bellies. He knew his time was short and not a time to be sad. Sitting in his chair, the aromas from the oven and Lucas singing Italian songs warmed his soul. He would smile and hum along eagerly awaiting a culinary twist.

Henri's body was frequently cold and Lucas kept the fire going and wrapped his grandmother's blanket around for comfort. On the small table next to his chair, Lucas set a warm tea with a cassia stick and croissant. He often said it was his favorite when he felt tired. A few months went by and Lucas needed to help his grandfather eat warm soup and small regular meals if there was an appetite. Lucas was twenty-five and Henri was into his seventies. Time had gone by quickly for the pair of them and life had been good.

Henri passed away in his home with Lucas by his side. Lucas felt what his grandfather was feeling when he moved to the country alone. Like his new friend Bailee, he was living in the footsteps of his deceased family, living the way they would have wanted it. Lucas kept the house and opened the business after Henri's funeral. He placed an ad in the local paper about the renowned chef loved by everyone. Many mourners attended. Since opening Café Henri, visitors had read the history of Lucas' family and what his grandfather left to carry on his amazing legacy.

After learning about Bailee's story and how death had changed so much for her and her family, Lucas pondered. He did not want loss to change who he was. Instead, he wanted to use his story to help Bailee with her journey to recovery and be happy again.

Henri had often encouraged, "A smile and love are at the end of the road to life. Without it, we have nothing to wake up to, no one to touch our heart. Smile at someone and they will mirror it back to you. *Donner l'amour et revoir l'amour.*" Give love and receive love. That was Henri's way. Lucas realized how he felt about Bailee. It wasn't the romance of France that made him feel that way, it was taught to him. It was not that there weren't bad times in his life. At one time, he tried to find his mother, unsuccessfully. His family had become the visitors to his café and those who loved his grandfather. Lucas knew it was important to leave a legacy too. Someday, he would do the same as Henri.

After Lucas got off the train and sent Bailee on her way back to her hotel that day, he walked into the café with a different step. It felt lonely in his kitchen without Bailee. He had never felt that way before. He used to feel invigorated by the banging of bowls and pots and bakers at work. He realized that her smile wasn't there to watch him create. Her presence was somewhere other than with him. It just wasn't the same. Was he in love or was this just loneliness coming back into his life? Each time Lucas poured and mixed flour or when he chopped vegetables, he kept thinking of Bailee. He pictured her holding his child in her arms. He was singing to her as she bounced a son or daughter on her hip. They were eating together as a family in the evening and holding the woman he loved safely in their bed at night.

The kitchen was still empty before the early morning light peeked through the windows as dawn approached. He stepped out of the kitchen and looked at the empty tables that would soon be filled with customers. He had a job to do and he was going to do it for Bailee. He would honor Henri for his love and patience, a grandfather who helped his grandson become the man he wanted. At that moment, Lucas realized he was deeply in love with Bailee.

Chapter 18

La Patisserie

Lucas took it upon himself to show Bailee some common and obscure places during her visit. She delighted being led through a tall building and looking over the top for an extended view of Paris. They consciously preferred to embrace their time together instead of her departure and noticed that it was harder to be apart. Even their mood would change when they were together again.

Near the café, she loved to sit and watch him interact with regulars. He would always look back and smile. It made her feel wanted. Observing him was like a show he was putting on just for her. Darting back and forth from tables to kitchen, he was precise and efficient. With or without food, she enjoyed Lucas in his finest environment.

During the days they spent together, he acted like a giddy schoolboy. She would take pictures of them at the fountains and Lucas would splash water into the air and make her laugh. She was encouraged to taste foods she was not familiar with and totally fell in love with everything that had butter. Trying new things had never been easy for Bailee. Lucas would describe the dishes beforehand to make sure she would give it a chance before prejudging. And desserts were always her favorite. She copied Lucas and tasted them slowly, expressing vocal delight.

When visiting The Louvre, they caught themselves walking side by side in rhythm. They both felt it. Strong friendship was turning into love. He naturally wanted to hold her hand but kept it to himself. He would not rush it. He was enjoying a new feeling of love for the first time.

"I have lived in France my whole life and have never been inside The Louvre," he admitted.

"Really? It's beautiful. Why have you never been here?"

"I have always felt that it was something that shouldn't be seen alone. Now that you are here, I have a reason. I can take it all in with someone who can love it too."

"It is incredible. Visiting Paris with you has been wonderful. I came here for one purpose and then I planned to go back to my life before I met you. When I became alone for the first time, I missed that closeness. Being with you, well, this was unexpected."

He stopped and turned to look at her as visitors passed by.

"Bailee, What have you been feeling? How do you feel about me?"

"Why does that question scare me?" she asked herself.

"You have nothing to fear when you are with me."

She hesitated for a moment and let the silence grow between them. He never took his eyes off of her while she pondered.

"I am feeling something for you, Lucas. You have been such a good friend while I have been here. When I look at you, I feel like I have been freed from my pain. I know that sounds so final, but I do."

He reassured her, "No, what you feel is real. I feel free from the loneliness I've had."

"I want to share this day with no one but you. If this is a dream, don't wake me. In my heart, we can only get better."

He hugged her and after releasing, stroked her cheek looking at every inch of her face. She looked down for a second and he lifted her chin back up to his face.

"Always have your eyes looking this way. Henri used to say, "*Looking down at the floor is not as beautiful as seeing the view God created.*"

"I like that."

Each time together, she experienced another small breakthrough. Bailee was breaking down her walls and becoming vulnerable. Fear had always held her back. This was a new sensation. She trusted Lucas and wanted to absorb everything around her. They spent parts of every day together.

"Tell me, who does the cooking in your family?" he quizzed as they walked into another gallery.

"It used to be my father. When my mom became too weak, he did his best to provide and did everything for us. When he got too depressed, I took it upon myself to clean and make meals. After my sister left home at seventeen, he lost all of the drive he used to have. Our family was not like yours. We never thought about food like you did. It was a way to survive. After Jen moved away, nothing was the same."

"What has changed now for you? After you return home, what will you take with you?"

"I wish it could be like this when I go home. I will take you and your spirit with me, everything you are and what you helped me see. I might be afraid to be without you."

"You will never lose me no matter where you go. It is true. For me, France will never be the same without you. But you, you are strong. I can see the changes in you."

"My sister used to ask me why I was so strong. She assumed that I never became sad or cried, losing our mother. I hid all that from Jen and Dad. I think I am like my mother, the strong person who protected the ones she loved. The only person I couldn't protect was Jen. Really, I don't think I could even protect my dad," she reasoned.

"Things happen out of our control. You shouldn't let that kill your search for happiness or keep you from love. But, what I feel for you, Bailee, is not something I want to go away. When you are back home, how am I going to go on without seeing your face or hearing your laugh? These are the things I fear."

"While I've been here, I have been thinking about how Jen would've felt if she found security and comfort here. I always thought I would be the one to erase her negative feelings and help her get what she strived for, real happiness."

"You look like you are living in her spotlight and that is okay. See it through her eyes. What would she want you to do to be happy? I think Jen would want you to follow your heart."

"Would that mean speaking my truth?" She felt her nerves give in. Bailee knew what the heart wanted and needed more than anything. She slowly explained, "Because my truth is that I love you."

He stopped and took her hand.

"You love me? I have been waiting for you to say those words."

He softly held on to her hand and then spoke again.

"I feel the same way." He looked at her with surprise and joy. "I want you to come to my café tonight. There is something special I want to do for you. Will you come?"

"Yes. Can you tell me what we are going to do?"

"*Non*. I want you to see me in my element. Be there after we close."

After their tour, she went back to her hotel to rest and freshen up. The smile never left her after bravely taking the chance to confess her love. She could not think of anything else but that beautiful moment near the Monet.

The café closed and the dining room and kitchen were cleaned and prepared for the next day. When the last server went home, Lucas went to lock the doors and saw Bailee waiting outside. She had dressed casually in jeans and a T-shirt. He waved her in and locked the door.

"Okay, why are we here? I have been going crazy wondering what we are going to do in an empty café."

"You are a painter and you love to create. We are more alike than you realize. So I am going to show you how our two worlds come together."

In the kitchen, she stood next to a long steel table and watched Lucas. He had worked part of the day and still had flour on his clothing. His dark hair curled around his forehead and he swept it back with his forearm.

After arranging several bowls, he reached for an apron, “Here, put this on.”

After she dropped it over her neck, he quickly knotted the ties. Bailee held her breath until he lifted his head and their eyes met.

After a moment, he turned his attention back to the table. Lucas was a natural in the kitchen. He flawlessly poured measured ingredients in the bowls and began to mix. When she saw the flour and butter, Bailee guessed it was some kind of dessert, one that would amaze her.

He put his hands on her hips. “You stand here. You are going to be the baker.”

“But I don’t know how to do that,” she said confused.

“Create. Use your imagination to make this dough. Think of what it can became and how beautiful it will be.”

She began to mix the butter and thought about how she had often baked for her father. She could see Chap watching over her without mentioning her mistakes. He always praised her, proud of her efforts. It was all that Chap had to make him smile. In Lucas’ kitchen, Bailee wanted to make him proud, working to get it just right.

“You have gone to a happy place, *oui*?”

“Yes. At first, I was afraid I might ruin it. But I do my best because my father believed in me.”

“I believe in you too, Bailee.”

She looked at his face closer. “I can see that.”

He had her lift the dough off of the table and grabbed a handful of fine flour. He shook it gracefully until the surface was covered.

"I call it snowing," he grinned. "Now this is perfect. Well, a little too perfect if you ask me." Lucas rubbed his fingers against her cheek, softly brushing flour on her face.

She placed the dough back on the floured table and began to work it. Lucas told her how his grandfather made it fluffy. He stood behind her and talked her through the steps of layering it delicately.

"Very good. You see, because you are an artist, you made something beautiful." He placed his hand on hers and her emotions took over. She was inside Lucas' beautiful world.

"I never thought I would ever do this with you. It feels dreamy," she admitted.

"No, Bailee. My beautiful Bay. You are not dreaming. I will always be here with you."

After putting her creation in the oven, Lucas turned his attention toward her. He wrapped his hands around her waist and lifted her onto the table. He did not release and she did not push him away.

His face came nearer and he whispered, "You are so much more than anything I could create."

He wasn't sure if he should get closer. With flour on his hands, he placed them on her face and studied her expression. She brought her lips softly to his and her hair fell onto his wrist. Their eyes closed. She never imagined falling in love so far from home.

"What has happened?" she whispered.

"You have found love."

"Yes, I have."

They held on to each other and he began to smile at her.

"What is it?" she pried.

"I have something I want you to try."

He went to the cooler and took out several desserts and placed small samples on a plate for her.

"Close your eyes. No looking. I want you to use all your senses to help you."

"Okay."

He lifted a fork to her mouth.

"Now, taste this, eyes closed."

She took her time tasting the sweetness and the savory flavors that awakened her senses.

"What do you taste?" he asked.

"Pear, apple, and mmm, butter."

"Very good. Taste the wine."

She sipped it slowly and tried a few more of the desserts.

"How do you feel?" Lucas asked.

"Wonderful. Each dessert makes me feel a different emotion. This one is happy and that one is pleasurable."

"Tell me what you taste in the wine."

"It has a buttery smoothness. I taste the oak barrel and some rich grapes with blackberry and currant."

"You are correct. It's amazing how wine is food's best friend and lover. They go good together and are as one. I never want food to be a sad experience. My grandfather put everything into his dishes and he taught me to enjoy life, because time on earth is short and we never know where life will take us."

"Your creations are like nothing I have ever experienced. In my heart, I am so thankful for your papa and what he taught you. Think about what you can pass on to your own family." She caught herself because a thought crossed her mind for a brief moment and felt herself blushing. "Oh, I'm sorry. Maybe you aren't thinking about that."

"No, I have always wanted my own family. There has never been anyone who cared to give me that privilege. With you however, there is hope for a bright future."

"I love that thought."

Lucas slid the pastry out of the oven and placed it onto a wooden board. The steamy aroma filled the kitchen.

"It still gets to me every time. Warm bread and pastry!" he mused. "Just grab a piece like this and rip it off. It always tastes best when it almost burns your fingers," Lucas grinned with ecstasy.

He made coffee and shared it as they sat on the prep table. Nibbling and talking in the café all night reminded him of Henri. Without his own family, he felt like he was living in Henri's shadow, the grandfather who never got over losing his beautiful Amie with stories of happy times. They talked in the café after the late hours. There was something about nights like that that made two souls feel like they could do anything. Love was alive.

Bailee wasn't thinking about home or leaving Paris. Her mind did suddenly become reminded of Jen. If her life wasn't cut short, she would have been released from the pain of abuse and she would have found her true love. A tear streamed down her face as she thought about what could have been.

"You are overcome with emotion, *Cherie.*"

"You were right. Remember when you said I was living my life as if I was Jen? The way I feel tonight is the way I wanted her to feel. I wanted her to find love, have children, to see my father holding them in his arms and laugh together. What my father didn't understand was that our mother was part of who we were. My father never had to worry about us forgetting her. I think he became sad because he couldn't hear her voice anymore. After Jen left, he couldn't hear her either. He lost all hope to be happy again."

"I would love to meet this man. There is still love and passion in his heart. I assure you, Bailee, he will find it very soon. You brought out the best in me and you would do the same for him."

"I have been afraid to find love because I never wanted to be hurt like he was. I distressed about losing someone I would love and end up like Dad. I needed to be strong. I avoided shedding tears and worked hard to keep my hope strong after they died. What I hadn't realized was that my strength was acting like my wall. The light touched my face when I met you."

"When Henri died, I lost hope. I have no family but his memories and the people at my café. That was all that kept me alive until I saw you sip your coffee. I saw someone beautiful and feisty," he cocked his head and smiled.

"That is something I will always carry with me. I kinda knew you liked me; sweet, creamy coffee and all."

"I can't say I felt the same way," he chuckled.

"I'm sorry about that."

"It was beautiful. There is no need to apologize. I found love, I found you."

It was getting late and neither wanted the evening to end. They sat near the dining area where an old couch leaned against the wall. She curled up next to him as he put his arm around her. He just listened to her talk about her life. He could see that she loved her family very much. She had the same passion as Lucas and it made him love her even more. She was surrounded by good food, a man who eased her fears and calmed her pain, and most of all, she was loved. She trusted Lucas and believed he had opened up about everything he had been through in his life. She would have given him everything if she could.

Lucas had not talked about past loves or Monique. Why did he hesitate to tell Bailee? While she was in his arms, he thought about revealing it, but was suddenly overwhelmed with guilt. The last thing he wanted to do was hurt her. He decided to be courageous and to come clean for her sake.

"Bay, I need to tell you something."

She yawned, "What? I should probably head back to my hotel. Can it wait until tomorrow?"

"It can wait. Let me walk you to the door."

Lucas was tired and the urge to sleep may have clouded his thinking. He saw a life with Bailee and telling her about Monique had the capacity to ruin that for him. But was it fair to keep it from Bailee? If she never knew, then she would be protected from heartache or fear.

"Lucas, there is nothing in this world that can top this night with you. Every time you take me on a new adventure, I see your heart and what you love and I know you truly care about me. Thank you for that," she said while touching his face.

"I don't want to think about what life would be like without you. For now, it's perfect where we stand."

He kissed her and locked the door. Bailee made her way along the well-lit streets to her car. Her mind was in ecstasy. France at any time of day was such a fantasy to her.

Lucas decided to sleep at the café. His thoughts were rolling around in his head and he got very little sleep. When the sun arose, he was ready to welcome his employees and guests to another day at Henri's Café. Lucas was in for the surprise of his life. An unexpected visitor would return and change his world.

Chapter 19

The Return of Monique

Bailee kept in touch with her father and was happy to learn he was feeling better. Brad was a giving friend and was always available for support. Bailee couldn't think of a better person to care for her father. Chap bought a corkboard like the one Jen had. Postcards from Bailee and several family photos were pinned in place. Bailee intentionally avoided informing him about Lucas. Since it had been only two weeks, she didn't know how to explain how she fell in love so quickly. She knew his first priority was that his daughter was safe.

With less than one week left until she returned home, she wanted to use those precious days to take in as much as she could. Each day she spent with Lucas was a memory she could lock away and save when it seemed like her days were grim thinking about Jen. Because she had such a good time getting to know Marie, she remembered the invitation her friend gave her to come and visit again with Lucas. Bailee pitched the idea to him and he gladly accepted. Any time they went someplace together, they held hands. Lucas mentioned that it was his favorite thing to do with her. It was a strong connection, keeping love close.

"It will be interesting to hear more stories about Henri. Marie has lived here twelve years and she knew of him," Bailee said.

"I am very happy to meet Marie."

He thought about how his relatives must have felt when they encountered true love. He could feel how she put a new step in his day. Everyone around him could see his happiness.

As Bailee turned up the lane, she pointed out Marie's cottage at the end. Stepping up to the walkway, she grabbed his hand and rang the bell.

"*Bonjour! Viens, entrer dans cette maison.* Come, enter this house," Marie welcomed.

When Marie opened the door, Lucas could smell her cooking. He inhaled and closed his eyes.

"There is nothing like the wonderful smell of fresh cuisine," Lucas commented.

"I knew you would notice," Marie remarked.

She took their coats and sat them down to some charcuterie items placed on a wooden board. She brought over three wine glasses and a bottle of Merlot. Marie noticed how close Lucas and Bailee were sitting as she poured.

"Is there something going on I should know?" Marie inquired.

They both looked at each other and just laughed.

"Should we tell her?" Bailee asked.

"Go ahead," Lucas encouraged.

"We fell in love."

"How did this happen?" Marie asked.

"It's hard to explain. I just left something at the café the first time I met him and I never realized what it was I was missing." Bailee's turned to look at Lucas.

"Well, I am happy you found each other. Being here together is a bit of a celebration."

Bailee felt the need to justify, "I know it's only been two weeks. My parents knew they loved each other when they were six. I'm just happy I gave Lucas another chance."

Lucas stood up to help Marie in the kitchen.

"Oh, no. You know as a chef you need to be the guest sometimes."

"C'est vrai." Lucas agreeing this is true.

"Bailee, have you talked to your father yet?"

"Yes. I called him and sent a couple of postcards. He's doing well."

"You should talk him into visiting France. I would love to meet him."

"I'm sure in time he will come around. He's been seeing a grief counselor and I'm happy to say, he's feeling quite a bit better."

"I know that feeling. I am a counselor, but after Jason and Jen died, I had to get some help. I'm happy to hear he's better."

They sat around the table swapping stories and laughing about the good times they had experienced. Even Bailee talked about her family's fun moments. Marie related some stories about Henri and his generosity to the community.

"Lucas, I remember when there was a family who didn't have much money or food. Henri made them a feast and then invited their neighbors to make it feel like a family event. Do you remember that story?" Marie asked.

"Ah, yes. The father thanked him by giving him two of his piglets."

"Did he keep the piglets?"

"No. He gave them to a friend who had a farm. The man's grandchildren loved them so much that they lived there for years," Lucas explained.

"What a wonderful story," Bailee admired.

Marie knew of other fond memories. She stopped by the café after she attended Henri's memorial. She grew very fond of Lucas and the endearing stories he told about his ancestors who loved food and family. She developed a maternal feeling she had been missing for a while.

Marie learned how to draw close to those who needed love and support from family, even if they were not related. To her, everyone she knew felt welcomed by her. When they talked about the ones they lost, vivid memories were still close. New experiences were now being made and they were on their way to making a happy life.

The wine had run out and Lucas and Bailee were ready to go back to the city.

They stood up together, "Marie, we appreciate your hospitality. Thank you for a wonderful evening."

"You are welcomed anytime."

They gave kisses on the cheek, saying their goodbyes in French.

The ride back to Paris was relaxing for Lucas. He amazed himself at how much he had never felt this kind of love for anyone, even Monique. While next to Bailee, he fell asleep resting his head on her shoulder. Before visiting Marie, Lucas thought about what Jean said earlier about Monique coming by the café many times to reconcile with Lucas. It appeared that she was staying away but tried calling many times. He never returned her calls, afraid to face her again knowing she would beg him to take her back. What he felt at the time was mistaken for love. He would not make that mistake again. He couldn't help but feel guilty for not telling Bailee about her.

Lucas remembered Monique as a young woman who had answered his ad for a server at Café Henri. She was beautiful. Her long brown hair and winning smile made it easy for Lucas to hire her. She was friendly, proficient, on time, and easily filled in for anyone who couldn't come in to work. There were many times when Monique volunteered to stay late and help Lucas clean. Some of the employees observed their relationship growing. It became more and more obvious when she openly began flirting. Since she was French like Lucas, they spoke their native language and lived her idea of the French lifestyle. She came from a good family but was a little spoiled. He shrugged off her opinionated comments about his country cottage, his grandfather and never riding the train. It was clear that he could never invite her to visit him, unlike Bailee. She persisted in looking for a flat in Paris for them, with his money, of course. Lucas wasn't much of a phone talker and when he didn't call often, Monique became upset. Lucas was handsome enough, but she wanted someone who would dote on her and offer her the life she had dreamed of. The air quickly went out of their time together. She began to use her time to search for others who thought more like her.

When Lucas told Henri that he wanted to marry Monique to keep her from leaving, Henri shook his head.

"That is no reason to marry someone. Real love is a stronger bond and it helps that love to keep growing. Real love pushes the whole world aside until it is only you two."

Lucas recalled times when they were closer emotionally. Love was very new to Lucas, and Monique was his first romance. For two years, they went through the ups and downs of a young relationship. As Lucas thought about proposing, he realized that marriage was difficult to prepare for and not to be taken lightly. Monique may have sensed his hesitation.

Lucas became increasingly conscious about Monique returning. What did she really want? When she made attempts to see him at work, he blew her off and she finally gave up her battle to get him back until that day.

She was dressed in her best, a ploy to possibly attract Lucas' attention and talk to her. She knew Jean and she just helped herself into the back of the kitchen. Jean knew exactly what she was after and tried to look extra busy to avoid her.

"Jean, where is Lucas?"

"What are you doing here? Only the staff is allowed back here and you know we are busy."

"Answer my question. Where is Lucas?"

"I don't know." He walked away finding another task.

Monique didn't listen to Jean and walked around the busy workers searching. His office was closed when he heard her knock. He opened the door, very surprised.

"Luc, I've been looking for you. I want to talk to you."

Monique barged in. Lucas went back to his desk and continued to fill out the supply form. He wasn't looking at her. "Monique, I thought we talked about this. I have nothing more to say and you wouldn't listen. Why do you keep trying to rekindle what we used to have?"

"I have been missing you. I know I was overbearing and my requests were unreasonable. I'm sorry and I want to come back."

He glanced up at her near the door.

"Why? You were the one who ended it. Remember, you wanted to be free from me and my efforts to make a happy life for us."

"I've gone through some changes and I just need what we built together."

He took a breath for courage and spoke clearly and slowly.

"I am not stupid. Any changes you have been through won't change this. I care about you as a human and I know you have feelings, but restarting love with you is foolish and is not going to happen."

Monique put her head down and began to explain why she returned.

"Luc, after we ended our love affair, I met someone. He loved me. He was decent and kind but I didn't love him. He wanted to care for me and give me everything I wanted to be happy. I agreed to marry him and then I..." She paused to think of the best way to present it. "I became pregnant."

He looked at her still unaffected by her news. It was not the reaction she hoped for. Maybe he would be more sympathetic if she continued.

"He was away for days working and I was left alone. The stress and loneliness took a toll on me and my emotions. I suffered a miscarriage and I almost died. My husband Ben, was not there to care for me and I resented him for not grieving with me. When I separated from him, he said that I hurt him. We just finalized our divorce and I have been so depressed. I have been reminiscing about all the wonderful times we have had. I misjudged you and I have changed."

He looked up into her deep brown eyes, searching for her logic.

He shook his head, "It's too late for that, Monique. I am in love with someone who is everything I dreamed of. We shouldn't have been together. It was wrong for you and me to think we were in love. This is what you do. You get it in your head that you want to be in love or be like those couples who have it all before you figured out who you are."

"How could you say that? I know I can make you happier than this woman can."

"You don't even know her. If you look at everything beautiful, that is who she is."

"Please, Lucas. I don't want to be alone anymore. You know me better than anyone. Give me a chance."

"I don't want to talk here anymore."

Lucas got up and led her out of the office into the hallway.

"Monique, this is the last time I am going to say this to you. We are never going to be together. I made myself clear after you hurt me and refused to communicate. Your coming here is entirely inappropriate. We are not going to make amends and it's not going to work. You killed every chance of getting love from me."

"Who is this woman who makes you believe she is your true love?" she asked.

Lucas knew better than to answer anything about Bailee.

"Why would it matter who she is?"

"You say she's beautiful, everything you ever wanted. That puts me in a bad light without any forgiveness for the mistakes I made."

"You're desperation makes you this way. I didn't want to hurt you, so I listened to your pain. I know you can find your way and make a happy life somehow. Just do it without me in it. I have found love, but she has nothing to do with my decision to let you go. I met her after getting the courage to move on from you."

"But you wanted to marry me; you told me you loved me. You never meant it?"

Just as Lucas began to answer, Bailee peeked her head into the kitchen and saw Lucas and Monique. She moved close enough to listen in. Monique stepped closer to Lucas.

"I did mean it when I said I loved you. I'm not a coldhearted person," said Lucas.

Monique put her hands on Lucas' shoulders and came close to his face. He put his hands on her arms to hold her away.

"I know you still care for me."

Bailee couldn't believe what she saw. Jean came around the baker's rack behind Bailee.

"Did you find him?"

When he turned and saw Monique and Lucas together, he looked at Bailee with wide eyes.

"Bailee, it's not what you think," Jean explained.

Lucas said nothing more to Monique. He pushed away from her emotional grip. Bailee watched and couldn't move. Monique turned to see her observers and came over to Bailee. She assumed she was the woman Lucas loved. A fire inside impelled her to be as vicious as she could be to the innocent woman who knew nothing about his past love.

"Jean, who is this?" Monique asked looking at Bailee up and down.

"This is Bailee. She is Lucas' friend." Jean heard his name and called to the kitchen. *"Je suis en route ! Pardon.* Monique, I suggest you leave now."

She ignored his request and did her best to sound entitled.

"I'm Monique, Lucas' girlfriend."

"Really? He never mentioned you."

"There is a reason for that. If you're thinking about taking him from me, don't. We were just talking about getting back together and you are in the way. He made it clear you were a waste of his time. This isn't the last time you will see me. Go back to where you came from."

Lucas saw them talking and hurried over. He knew Monique would get revenge by hurting Bailee. As she walked away smiling, Bailee felt the anxiety growing throughout her body.

"Bailee!" Lucas reached out to touch her arm to prevent her from turning away.

"I'm leaving! I saw you with that woman. Why didn't you tell me about her?"

"I wanted to. She is someone from my past. I'm not getting back with her. Believe me."

"I heard you two talking. The fact that you never revealed her to me sickens me."

"It's over, it's been over."

"Is it? She said you two are getting back together."

"No, that's not true."

He came close to her and she instinctively backed up.

"Don't come near me. I thought I could trust you."

Bailee made up her mind that the café was not a place for her to be. She turned to exit. Maybe Paris was not for her either. Her mind was in a place she suddenly wasn't used to. She wasn't thinking clearly and she didn't care.

"Let me tell you what she wanted. Please, Bailee don't go." He begged to closed ears.

She didn't look back and fought the urge to run. The words of Monique were messing with her mind and all she could think about was how stupid it was to fall for someone so soon. Lucas stepped outside the café to glimpse her walking across the street. After Jean found Lucas, he wrapped his arm around him.

"I have to fix this," Lucas said.

"Let it rest for now. Maybe after the emotions calm down, talk to her tomorrow."

Lucas could do nothing but go back to his office feeling helpless. He started to wonder why Bailee wouldn't believe him and how true their love really was. Since there was little more he could do, he decided to go home early and patiently wait for the next chance to meet with Bailee.

Walking in to his empty cottage, it felt oddly cold and instinctively brought more firewood inside. Feeling the need for more heat, he unfolded his grandfather's blanket and sat in front of the fireplace. He recalled Bailee standing in that very spot. After warming soup from the night before, he poured it into a mug and wrapped his fingers around it for warmth. Lucas thoughts began to race and panic, fearing the worst. He was afraid that the love he had waited for his whole life would leave. Without her, he would have missed out on all the love he saved, the same love he refused to give Monique. Since Henri passed, he had lived alone and his loneliness became more evident without Bailee. He had never cared about it before. He wanted and needed the warmth and comfort only Bailee could give, and he needed it most at that moment. It was hard to rest that night. His thoughts swirled about what he would say to win her back. It was a long night for Lucas.

In a Paris hotel room, Bailee was in tears. She thought this was exactly what she wanted and what happened that day was what she feared the most. She would close her eyes and feel Lucas' hand in hers. She could feel his kiss and hear his laughter. The flood of happier times played over and over in her mind. She wanted to run into his arms and hear his reasoning, but fear kept her away. There was just too much hurt in her life to trust him. Was he trustworthy? What else had he not told her? How many Moniques were out there? She knew if she talked to her father, he would have an answer as to what she should do. She anticipated the, "I told you so," speech because of how young she was. Chap often had good advice. Maybe she was overthinking it because of the pain in her heart for the man she loved. Her good judgement was being clouded by guilt and the thought of never seeing Lucas again. Why was that woman so heartless and why would Lucas be with her? What could she have offered him? She had to stop thinking and relax her mind. After taking a hot bath, she decided to call her father.

"Hey, Dad."

"Bailee, it's good to hear from you!"

“I miss you and I want you know I’m coming home early.”

“I thought you weren’t due until next week. What happened?”

Bailee couldn’t answer.

“Bay, what is it?”

“I feel heartbroken. I met someone while I was here and it all just fell apart today. He was the one. I fell in love hard and now everything hurts.”

“Oh, Bailee. I’m sorry. Do you want to talk about it?”

“It’s hard to talk it out. I saw him with an old girlfriend.” Bailee realized it was too difficult to provide more details, even if it was to her father. “I don’t think I can talk about this over the phone, Dad.”

“Okay. I understand you are hurt. If you want to come home, I will be here. You leave when you’re ready.”

As much as she wanted to talk about what Lucas meant to her, she held back. There was just too much to explain and she wasn’t in a place to do that. Chap felt sad for her. His heart ached because he wanted to help. Hearing his caring voice did help. She could feel his support. He thought a little advice may give her the courage to mend what went wrong.

“Bailee, can I say something?”

“Yes, Dad.”

“Sometimes things are not always as they seem. Sometimes your mom and I argued with each other until we discovered that it wasn’t really important. It’s a love thing. If you get a chance, talk to him. If you are in love, it will work out. Try to hear his side and go from there. Don't let bad feelings brood."

"I understand what you're saying. I can talk to him." She thought about it, knowing the man who gave everything still cared enough to guide her thorough her toughest times. After they finished their conversation, Bailee went to bed with an eased mind.

The next morning, Lucas decided to stop by her hotel room. He arrived early enough in case Bailee planned to take an earlier flight. She came to answer the door.

"Bailee, I want to talk. I couldn't sleep all night thinking about what you must have went through. There are so many things I want to say to keep you here with me. Please let me into your heart."

"You can come in."

They sat down and Lucas tried to be sincere as possible.

"I want to go first," she said. "I felt like my world came to an end yesterday when I saw you with Monique. Maybe your explanation is genuine, but I'm hurt you didn't tell me about her."

"That was a mistake. I should have told you sooner. Monique means nothing to me. That's what I was telling her when you showed up. She wants it to be the way we used to be. I told her that I came to life when I met you."

"This was not in my plans. I came here for Jen and I selfishly fell in love. Why did I do something so stupid?"

"I would never hurt you. What else can I say to make you believe me?"

"Nothing. I don't know what to believe. I made a mistake thinking this was going to work. Jen was the reason I was here and then I made it about you. I completely forgot about her when I met you. I feel so guilty about it."

"You are more like that glass vase than your realize."

"Why would you say that?"

"You need to be filled with love and that is what I gave to you. Now you want to empty us because of a misunderstanding? If leaving is how you cope with sadness, then go. I am willing to beg on my knees and show you how much I love you. I want to prove that you can trust me. I understand that you came here for Jen. Being together helped you cope with her death and you made your peace with it. I am not replacing your sister."

"You were not the reason I forgot Jen! I purposely gave in to satisfy my selfishness. I never want to forget what she meant to me."

"You don't have to forget her. That is not what I am asking you to do. If I had a past love, that is all it was, the past. I was honest with you about everything. This is something special for the both of us. I'm not sure I can ever go back to my life without you in it. I want to be back in your arms."

Bailee quietly walked to the door and opened it. Lucas got the hint. He was expected to leave.

Bailee wondered aloud, "I know you wanted so much from us, but I don't know what to do after meeting this woman who still loves you."

"She thinks she loves me. She is the one who is selfish."

"All I want to think about is Jen."

"Jen is gone, but I can help you keep her memory alive. No one will give you that support like I will. Don't throw it away, Bailee."

"I'm leaving tomorrow. Please, don't come by again or say goodbye. I couldn't bear it."

She began closing the door as his sad eyes tried to understand.

"This can't be it. You don't mean it."

"Please leave, Lucas."

Lucas was distraught. Bailee wasn't able to give him a chance. She refused his cries for redemption and couldn't hear him out. Bailee was wrong to not hear the whole truth. She wasn't thinking clearly enough to just jump back into Lucas' arms and forgive. She had never experienced that part of a healthy relationship before. Time might heal the open wound. She was not sure when or if she would change her mind.

Before Bailee made her flight, she wanted to see Marie again. She was at the gallery that day.

"Do you want to tell me what happened?" Marie pried.

"It's so complicated and I was just so hurt when I saw her with her arms around him. He made no attempt to push her away."

"Sounds like you didn't hear the whole conversation. I don't think Lucas intended to hurt you. He didn't even know you were at the café. What can I do to help you feel better?"

"I can't trust him. I'm torn between forgiving him and letting him go."

"Everyone wants to let go at first to get relief from the aching. It's easier than facing it. You may just need some time. Knowing Lucas, I have no doubt you will have him back in your life again."

"By then we may be on different paths. We live in different countries and life can change everything. I just have no hope that it can work it out."

Bailee promised Marie that she would visit again sometime. She knew she needed to think things through. She gave her a hug and held onto that embrace as long as she could to feel the closeness and love. Bailee would miss her and everything France meant to her.

Lucas tried calling Bailee and it automatically went to voicemail. After several attempts, he started to appear needy and he stopped trying. Bailee waited at the airport and when it was time to board, she looked back with sadness that she wasn't staying. As the plane lifted off the runway, she realized there was no turning back. Bailee was on her way home and she was leaving Lucas behind.

After a long flight, Chap met Bailee at the airport. It felt like years since he had seen his daughter. He ran to her arms and she began to cry. Chap pressed his face into her hair and just held on tight. She needed that embrace and Chap could see that Bailee was more than a little lovesick.

"Let's get you home," Chap suggested as he helped her with her bags.

It was quiet in the car on the way home as she stared out the window. Everything she saw felt odd, it had changed somehow. She was used to the little shops, old buildings and beautiful sights that came with seeing Paris firsthand. Most of all, she missed talking about food and watching Lucas make croissants. She wasn't sure how she would get back to herself again. Chap suggested she stay with him for a few days. She thanked him for the offer but preferred to be in her own home. She assured him she would be alright. As Bailee walked into her studio, her eyes fell upon the vase. Sunlight refracted through it and spilled onto the floor. She realized that it wasn't reasonable to think about Jen all the time. She did fulfill what she went to Paris to do. Jen would have been proud of her and maybe she would have told her it was foolish to leave him and should go back to him.

"Jen, I'm sorry I let you down. I came to France to honor you and find out why you were so sad. I feel so guilty I couldn't save you. Because I fell in love, I neglected to think about you first. I love you, Jen. I will always love you."

When Chap brought her bags in, he informed Nan of what he knew. She was ready to catch up on how things went in France, gossip and all. Nan cared about Bailee and the two of them had a special trust that made her feel comforted and loved.

"Bailee, it's Nan," she said as she knocked on the door.

"I'm so glad to see you. I missed you so much."

"I spoke with your father. Out with it. What happened?"

"Out of all the people I know, you would understand more than anyone."

"I've had my share of love and heartache."

Bailee related her experiences in France and then about Lucas. Nan listened intently and smiled at some of the stories that inspired Bailee. When she told her about the heartache, Nan took Bailee's hand and listened to the pain she felt. But Nan could also hear there was still love inside her. Nan was old enough to know what true love was like and when someone was deceiving. She couldn't see Lucas being that kind of person.

“My dear, could it be that you were a little presumptuous? You acted on fear, protecting yourself. Am I wrong?” Nan’s piercing eyes asked.

“I, well, I don’t think I did.”

“This man was willing to beg for your love. That is not the sound of someone who wants to be with another woman.”

“Did I make a mistake?”

“I’m not the one to answer that question. You went to France to honor Jen. You did that whether you wanted to believe it or not. It wasn’t that you put Jen aside to fall in love, you kept her close. But you also let someone in who helped mend what you lost. I am sure that Jen would’ve wanted that for you.”

Bailee realized Nan was right and she broke down. She didn’t believe Lucas should ever forgive her or take her back. Nan could feel her pain and put her comforting arms around her.

“Hush, my love.” She rocked her in her arms. “I truly believe Lucas could never stop loving you. You have to stop torturing yourself with those thoughts.”

“I want to talk to him but...”

“Your heart will tell you when it’s time to make that move. I think he’s hanging on for dear life waiting for you to come back.”

“You really think so?”

Nan nodded and wiped Bailee’s tears. No one could deny she was still in love.

Lucas shoved every bit of his sadness and concentrated on work. He commented on how the recent quality of his creations were disappointing to him. Everything lost its zest and flavor. Jean could see that he wasn't the same since Bailee left. Lucas walked the same places the two of them went to. In his mind, the city had lost its spark. He remembered when Bailee told him how difficult it was to visit Paris alone. He felt that same feeling without her. He wasn't meant to be without someone anymore. After work, he came home to prepare a small meal for himself. The house was warm and he heard someone at the door. He smiled until he saw who it was.

"Monique, why are you here? Haven't you caused enough trouble?"

"I came by the café but you had already left."

"You are not allowed to see me at my café. You don't even like to come to my home."

"Where is your precious Bailee? She is gone, *oui*?"

"*Oui.* What did you say to her?"

"It doesn't matter. I sent her away and that was all we needed."

"Are you insane?! What did you do?"

"I told her that you and I are back together. I know if you just let me prove it, you will love me again."

Lucas put his hands onto his head, in disbelief.

"Monique, you are so low. How could you do that to her? What will it take to get you to understand that I love Bailee. I would never hurt her like you did."

She felt defeated in his words. That was not supposed to be the end of her plan. She was trying to come up with the words to save herself.

"Luc, I never fought for us. I never made the effort to try and save what we had. I am begging you. This

American girl you say you love, cannot give you what I can. We have years of history."

"There was something my grandfather said that helped me make wise decisions and guide my life in the right direction. He said, "Walk away from the sparks before the fire causes pain. Never look back on what could have been and do not walk in the path of sadness." He continued on as she looked away.

"What we had actually made me unhappy because I wanted to be in love. I have to let you go. Have the life you want and please, do it without me. Goodbye, Monique."

He kindly walked her through the doorway. She could think of nothing to say or do to change his mind. He was acting like a man who knew what he wanted and knew how to get it. She knew he was right and had to accept his goodbye. She turned on the walk and whispered a soft, 'goodbye, Luc.'

As she walked to her car, his mind flashed back to the image of his mother leaving. He was helpless back then. He had become a man who could withstand adversity. Although losing another person in his life, it surprised him. He did not feel weak. He was ready for any challenge life would throw at him.

Two days later, Lucas returned to work and Jean handed him a note left by Monique.

"What is this?"

"She came by and left it for you."

Lucas sighed and went into his office to open it, expecting to find another plea.

My Dearest Luc,

I know you asked me to leave you alone and I have to respect your request. This is breaking my heart because of my ways; I lost the greatest love I could have ever had. I had a glimpse of our future. All my life I wished to end my loneliness and made some selfish choices. After losing my child, I hoped you would fill my empty heart. I can see that you are truly in love and you fought to prove that she is the only one for you. I wanted you to look at me the same way. I can see it in your eyes that she saved you. You probably did the same for her. I wanted that so badly and I went as far as I could to steal that from her. I wanted her to hate you, I wanted what she had. I wanted her to leave and never return so that you would know how I feel. Instead, you protected and nurtured her. When you look at her face, she will be glad you went to battle for her.

I thought if I begged with all my might, you would see the desperation in my pleas, in the sound of my voice, and you would just run into my arms and tell me, "It will be alright." After I left your home, I pondered, 'Where can I go now that I will never see you again?'

Someday you will be just a memory. That's not true to my heart, but it is what has to be. I really believed you would take me back. I'm not sure how long it will take to get over you.

I am staying with my parents until I can afford to live on my own. They are willing to help me get on my feet. My father is now the man I must depend on to be there for me.

I hope you have a good life with Bailee. I'm sad it won't be me holding your hand or kissing you goodnight. Someday a man may come into my life and rescue me like you rescued Bailee.

Goodbye my love, Monique.

When Lucas finished reading the letter, he sighed. He was released from the grip Monique stubbornly held on to. Even if Bailee never returned to him, he would be glad that he met a woman who taught him how to love. It was his time with her that strengthened and fueled his courage to let go of what held him down. For the moment, he had no expectations of his love returning to France or speaking to him again. His heart would have a deep hole. No other love could know what she meant to him and stand in her place.

Chapter 20

I'll Never Let Go

It had been six months since Bailee left France. She poured herself into her art and assisted local artists, avoiding contact with Lucas. When Chap brought up the subject, she just shook her head without a word. He got the hint and didn't bring it up again. He knew she still had deep feelings for Lucas and did not know why she couldn't admit it. He was secretly hoping she would just get on a plane and run to him. Chap would find the right time to approach her decision.

In the gallery, Nan watched Bailee's focus intensify. She worked long and hard until exhausted. Her mood was somber and she started nodding off at work. She could see herself in Bailee and didn't want her to make the same mistakes she made when it came to love and healing from a broken heart. Nan put her feelings away when she lost the love of her life. If she could go back, she would have never left France and she would have started over repairing what was torn apart. She knew she couldn't intervene and Bailee needed to learn how to do this on her own. Besides, Bailee knew Nan wanted her to believe that Lucas had her best interests at heart. Fear keeps us from looking at the real issue and seeing beauty amongst all the flaws. There was something good between Bailee and Lucas. He saved her. What would life be like if she never went to France or met Lucas? Her life took on a new meaning and she can finally put the grief she felt for Jen and Caryn to rest. Lucas taught her that. It wasn't that she couldn't do it without him, it was better that she had him by her side. He wanted more from their friendship. He wanted to make a memory with her that would last their whole life. Lucas came into Bailee's life at the perfect time.

Nan suggested Bailee take time off to rest before the next art show and she decided to go to bed early. That night, she had a disturbing dream.

She was outside of the Twin Towers. It was crumbling and she could hear Jen crying out to her. The muffled cries for help got louder and she attempted to run inside. Lucas grabbed her by the hand. When she tried to shake his grip, he held on tighter.

"Bailee, help me!" The cries were vague and sounded muffled. She could hear other people crying for help but Jen's voice was recognizable.

"Stay with me," Lucas begged standing outside the chaos. He held out his hand and showed persistence.

She was torn and could not decide. She tried calling out to Jen but her guilty voice would not reply. As the tower started to collapse, Bailee watched the building tumble in slow motion as Lucas pulled her back to safety. Bailee could only say, *no,* over and over. She let go of Lucas and walked onto the rubble to see Jen lying there, wearing the bracelet she loved. All she could do was cry silent tears and whisper, *'I'm sorry, Jen. I'm so very sorry.'* When she turned to see if Lucas was still near, thick dust blocked her view. The air cleared briefly revealing a shadow of the man she loved and gave away. Lucas was in the arms of Monique and they quickly disappeared behind another cloud. All that was left was destruction. Anxiety filled her, realizing he was out of her life. When she tried to go after him, screaming his name, she awoke with her heart rapidly pounding.

She turned on the light for clarity. After getting out of bed and getting her composure, she walked over to the vase. Bending down to take a closer look, her fingers stroked the side, appreciating its unique design. She knew she still loved Jen and the vase was just as beautiful. All those times that Jen noted Bailee never cried or experienced sadness, wasn't true. She was trying to show bravery and strength, hiding what she really felt. Being without Lucas highlighted what she was holding in all those years, taking care others instead of herself. What would Jen feel like if she saw her sister give way to tears while in pain? Bailee felt shame for not showing her feelings in front of Jen after their mother's death.

Jen would have said, "You don't have to give up your love for Lucas just for me, my sister; not even for my memory."

She nestled herself back under the comforter. Laying in her soft bed felt indescribably empty. She pictured a fire flickering within its hearth and the one she loved sleeping nearby.

Was that a breakthrough for Bailee? Could it give her the motivation to go back to Lucas?

Bailee came to see Chap after work. Brad was visiting.

"Hey, Brad."

"Good to see you." He came in for a hug.

"Your dad was telling me how much you miss France. Have you thought about going back someday?"

"I have. That's why I'm here. I want to talk to Dad about something."

"Say no more. I gotta get going. You two have a nice visit."

"Thanks, Brad. We'll get some dinner next week," Chap suggested.

"My place."

"You got it."

"I've always thought of him like an uncle. He's the best," Bailee admired.

"He's been good to me these past years. He came by to give me the news he's finally getting married and wants me to be his best man."

'That's good news. Brad has always wanted to be married again. I'm happy for him."

"What brings you here, honey?"

"I have been thinking a lot, maybe too much. I am exhausted and I need a break. Nan suggested a mini vacation. Are you up for it?"

"I like the sound of it. Where are you thinking, the cabin?"

"That is the perfect place to get away."

On the way up, they both marveled at the season's color changes. Deciduous trees were losing their foliage, standing out amidst the evergreens. Bailee rolled her window down and inhaled the crisp air. The countryside had similar characteristics to her European experience. Her mind relaxed and began to open up. There was so much to express. Bailee began to relate her moments in France. When she got to the events at Café Henri, Chap's delight grew. She seemed to know quite a bit about a man she had just met. It reminded him of his own love.

The gravel road ended at the cabin littered with fallen leaves. Bailee loved the way the air smelled. After an early morning walk, the mist was lingering, cleaning the air with freshness. She could see the rays peeking through the trees and she took it all in with a big breath. It felt good to have her childhood memories surface with the man who gave her the love she needed. He did his best to be sure his girl rejoiced and knew she was blessed having Chap as a father.

Chap raised his arms up and stretched, "This place just gets better every time I'm up here. How does it make you feel?"

"Well, it does feel smaller, but everyone says that about childhood memories. I used to think our backyard was huge."

Before bringing their bags inside, Chap grabbed her hand and walked her down the path to the lake. He thought about taking the canoe out and enjoying the water. Chap always thought paddling onto the water was relaxing.

"Almost as good as the old days. We had some great times up here, didn't we?" Chap reminded.

"It seems so quiet up here without the whole family."

"Yep, it's just you and me."

"What do you think Mom and Jen would say right now?" Bailee asked.

She closed her eyes and pictured the three of them holding hands and giggling as they jumped into the cold water. It felt good. There was no reason for sadness by either of them. They took back their power from that emotion and could find balance in their past and future.

As the sun settled between the trees, they sat on the front porch watching dragonflies skimming the water. They could see fish leaving little splashes as they jumped for their evening meal. The osprey and various birds were a delight to see coming out of their nests to enjoy the sunshine. The last of the sun glistened on the water as it circled around, awaiting the next day. It was a perfect time for a father and his beloved daughter to talk things out.

"Dad, I know you have been wanting to talk to me about my relationship with Lucas ever since I came back."

When she turned toward him, her eyes sparkled like the lake surface. He had seen that same look from his own wife.

"As a father, I care about my daughter, but the decision to mend things with Lucas is up to you. I think you know what you should do."

"I started forgetting about Jen while I was with him. When I thought Lucas lost his love for me, I dropped every hope that it could be fixed."

"I know you don't want to believe it, but nothing was broken. You think you did the right thing. Looking back, was it really? Be honest. And as far as forgetting Jen, you didn't. You are moving on and coming to terms with her death. What's wrong with that?"

"I...I think it was the right thing to do at the time. It may have been wrong to leave without listening to everything he had to say. But emotionally, I didn't feel safe."

"You told me stories about his grandfather and how he learned to be just like him. He put in all of that hard work to open and run a restaurant, caring for thousands of visitors and his employees. They became like family. Bay, that love is in his veins and what he feels for you is solid. I doubt that would ever go away."

"What if it's too late? What if I go back to France and he is with Monique?"

"Or what if he is waiting for you to come back? If he told you he doesn't love this Monique, then he was speaking his truth. You have to go with that."

"I'm scared."

"You don't have to be. I haven't met this man, but I think he is likely very forgiving. You should give him a chance."

"And if he doesn't want me back? What should I do?"

"I don't think you should hold your breath on that question. You can let your guard down, Bay. It's going to be okay."

"You always have the right thing to say when things go wrong. Thanks, Dad."

"I think there is someone who is waiting for you to take a trip to Café Henri. What do you say?"

"You are right. I should make plans to see Lucas."

He hugged her with all the love a father could give, proud of her giving love the chance it deserved. She was going into the unknown with support from her father. That evening, they sat around the campfire that faced the lake. It was evident that they were no longer sad about their losses. Time helped them figure it out. They could talk about Jen and Caryn, recalling happier times and even some humorous moments. Those are the memories that counted the most.

Lucas was in his office putting in orders for the month. Jean came by to tell him that one of the servers called in sick and he could stay late to help out if needed. As Jean shut the door, he walked toward the entrance to the café. There she stood smiling at him.

"Bailee! I haven't seen you in months. When did you arrive?" Jean asked.

"Last night. Is Lucas here?" She was nervous and it showed in her voice.

"*Oui.* He's in his office. Would you like to go in?"

"No. Can you bring him out? Don't tell him I'm here."

He leaned forward, "You know, Lucas hasn't been the same since you left. I never lost hope that you would return but he doesn't believe it. It makes me glad you are here to show my good friend how to be happy again."

"I love him. I will never leave him again."

"Thank you, Bailee. You are truly a beautiful person."

She smiled as he turned to get Lucas.

"There is someone here to see you."

"Jean, I'm very busy today. Who is it?"

"See for yourself."

"Can't you just tell me?"

As Lucas rounded the corner from his office, he looked at Jean strangely. Nearing the entrance. he saw her and stopped with amazement.

"Bailee," he sighed.

"Hello, Lucas."

"It has been so long." He was finding it hard to gather his emotions, "How are you?"

"I'm good, better. I had a lot to think about while I was away. My father and I spent some time together and he gave me some advice."

"What did he advise? Did he encourage you to come to France?"

"He nudged me. I was hesitant but he helped me see where I left my heart."

"If you are like me, you have never felt a sadness like this before. If it wasn't for Henri and his wisdom, I couldn't have gotten through it."

"I'm sorry for that. I left in fear. I should have listened to you." She looked down for a moment and drew courage, "Lucas, am I too late? Are you with Monique?"

"No. She has to find her own life. Whatever we had so long ago was not love. I realized what true love is the day I met you."

"Is there a place in your heart for forgiveness?"

"I forgave you the moment you got on that plane and left me." Lucas suddenly realized customers were pressing against them to get in. He pointed outside to the corner table. "Let's take a seat over here." He continued. "Tell me what made you come back?"

"Remember when Marie said I left something at the café when I first met you? I felt that way when I went away. I should have known better."

"I had so many thoughts. I'd stay awake at night thinking about what our children will look like, what would it be like to grow old with you and what would we fight about."

She smiled at that, “What else did you think about?”

“How beautiful my daughter will be because of her mother. She will love to pick flowers and dance, walk the country side with us. She will learn to cook and have the passion, just like me.” He took a deep breath and continued, “Henri left more than a legacy with me. He left his love with me. His daughter didn’t love him enough, but that didn’t hinder him from loving me. Because of that, I will never stop giving to my children and most of all, to you.”

“I want all of it. I want everything Henri gave to you. I will share it with you if you are ready.”

“I am ready. Bailee, I promise to always love you. No one will come between us.” He spread his arms out wide and imitated his papa, “France welcomes you. This is your home.”

The more Bailee thought about it, the more she wanted it as her permanent home. Marie must have seen herself in Bailee when she first moved to Normandy.

“Lucas, my heart made France home a long time ago. I know this is where I belong.”

He moved his face closer and let her kiss him. As they did, Jean quietly brought some servers around. After their embrace they all clapped for the two. Surprised, they could only grin. Both were true to the one they loved with no reason to waiver. It was forever. What was misunderstood was mended with love and understanding. That was what they wanted and needed. Jean put everyone back to work. Then, Lucas leaned over and said something in Bailee’s ear. “You can put whatever you want in your coffee as long as you are with me.”

She laughed back, “It’s fine just the way it is.

Chapter 21

You Are My Home

Chap knew the inevitable would happen when Bailee flew back to France. He could see how she wasn't the same after discovering her love. He realized that Bailee, who was deeply in love, belonged there. It would leave him alone, not like his loss with Jen and Caryn. Bailee no longer hid her feelings and began trusting again. It was a happier time for Chap. Even though he wanted to keep Bailee close by, he had to let his daughter go and live a happy life.

The weeks she had spent with her love were the happiest she ever had. Still sitting at the café table, her mind raced with arrangements needed to make France her home. Bailee thought of Nan, the gallery, her father, and whatever legal requirements existed. It was important to talk to Lucas about her newfound plans. He was always reasonable and she was learning to rely on his advice that wisely came from Henri.

"Lucas, I can't go back home. I need to be here with you. Is that selfish of me to feel that way?" she asked.

"I don't think so. Have you told your father?"

"I think he knows. When we were at the cabin together, he looked at me when I talked about you and my experiences here in Paris. I could see the look on his face and he told me what he felt without saying a word."

"Does that scare you?"

"I thought it would, but no."

"You need to go back to get everything arranged. When will you go back to California?" he asked somberly.

"Soon. I don't want to put a time on it." She leaned in. "I want to take in as much of you as I can. I learn something new about you every day we're together."

"Because of you, I will never be alone again."

He tenderly closed the gap and kissed her soft lips. He could feel her love surrounding him. Neither wanted that new feeling to disappear. Love had grown and Lucas' past generations would have been proud of him. Their legacy would carry on within him throughout the years.

Feeling obliged to go back to San Marino, Bailee checked her bags at the front desk and observed Lucas watching the planes ready to board, his hands in his pockets. She walked behind him and wrapped her arms around his waist.

"What are you thinking about?" she asked tenderly.

"How much I hate goodbyes. After you get on that plane, I will be without the breath that keeps me alive."

"I will be back in your arms soon." She turned him around to face her. She noticed his eyes were full of conflicting emotions, making it harder for her to leave. She would do anything to make him happy.

“Please do not be sad. This will be the last time we will have to be apart. You will never have to shed another tear for this reason.”

“I wanted these days together to be an eternity. It went by too quickly and I can’t say goodbye.”

As he expressed his thoughts, she placed her palm on his cheek. She let him say everything he was feeling and get out what he needed to say to the woman he loved.

“Bailee, my life has not been perfect. I have made many mistakes and I have tried to turn sadness into a cheerful place after Henri died. He helped me get to this point in my life and now that you are here, I can never be the same. I wish he was here to see how much I have grown and how being in love has made me feel.”

They could hear the last call to board her flight. Bailee stepped back and grabbed her bag reluctantly.

“I have to go. I will not say goodbye.” She just whispered, *Mon coeur t’emportera avec moi, mon amour.*

“Your French has gotten better. My heart will take you with me too.”

He couldn’t help it and pulled her into a warm embrace and held on as long as he could. Bailee finally tore herself away and smiled. She turned and briskly walked to the gate. He couldn’t move until she disappeared from sight. With heavy feet, he walked out of the airport and hailed a taxi to the train station.

When Lucas walked into his little home, he began looking around, thinking about changes he needed to prepare for. Plans began to formulate in his head to expand the house for more space. Without eating, he started going through his things and cleaning his home. He went out to the back of the cottage and surveyed the undeveloped land. The sun was nearing the horizon and cast shadows across the meadow. Henri had left him about ten acres that had been in its natural state. He wanted a garden to tend with fresh herbs and vegetables. Henri said that the lower area had the richest soil and would take less water. It only needed some fencing and a gate. He thought about his family raising chickens, rabbits, a few goats, and sheep. He could picture them roaming the property, eating all of the scrubby bushes. He remembered Bailee's love of cheese from the sheep's milk. She would love the animals and they would be a great complement to the land. Bailee also loved flowers and the green fields of Normandy. An idea excited him to make his home look the part. The pain of watching her leave left him the more he thought about how his place would look after renovation. Lucas knew of a contractor near his home who might help with the project. It would be his largest surprise for Bailee. Just thinking about filling the home with children made him grin from ear to ear. It was a marvelous thought and he couldn't wait to get started on his home project.

Bailee came home and put herself into her work and sold most of her paintings. Nan looked in on her as she was packing up some of the smaller art pieces that were special to her.

"When you went back to France you found your calling. You are moving to France to be near the one you love," Nan admitted sincerely.

Bailee stood up and came near, "He's my home. Are you going to be sad when I leave?"

"Of course, I'll be sad. I hate goodbyes too. Your experience with Lucas has changed me as well."

"How do you mean?"

"I have been thinking. I should go back to France and make some new memories. Thank you for sharing with me what real love is like. I kept to myself all these years when the man I loved left me. I wasted those years and I did not want that for you. I have been a little stubborn, and now I have so much regret."

"You never have to fear that you will lose me. Maybe going back to France will give you that new start. I will go with you on your journey to breaking free of your regret."

"Someday I will see that my heart has healed and take that step."

Bailee loved Nan so much. She was leaving the gallery for a new life. Nan had a lot of friends but no one could measure up to what she had with Bailee. She knew this young woman needed a mother figure and Nan had been perfect for the job. There was no question that their closeness would last.

That night, Bailee packed her photo albums, childhood drawings, yearbooks, her poetry book, and the glass vase. When she looked at the vase, she no longer obsessed about Jen. Her joy came from inside that matched her outer beauty. Jen may have never had the opportunity to live in France with Marie, but her memory lives on with happy times together. While she had the vase with her, she had never filled it with anything except the notes Jen pinned to her corkboard in New York. When Bailee had a positive thought or a poem, she would throw it in the vase. It was where she stored her valuable memories. The vase was finally being filled with love. Bailee was free of the misery and sadness of losing Jen. The glass vase came to be used to display joy. Flowers would have been the perfect way to say, "*I truly loved you, Jen.*"

Bailee had another guest at her door.

"Do you have time for a visit?" Lilly asked.

"Lilly! I sure do. Come in."

"I see you have most of your things packed. How are you feeling about moving all the way to France?"

"I feel so good. Earlier, Dad and I talked about the possibility of me leaving. He figured it out before I did. I guess he could see it in me."

"Well, with the love of your life waiting patiently, why wouldn't you go?"

"Oh Lilly, I will come and visit. I loved going to our cabin and I don't want to miss out on our family gatherings."

"We enjoyed having you. I would love to meet Lucas someday and thank him."

"He makes everything so wonderful. I know when people are in love and it's all new, they say that. They think the person they fell for is perfect. But I will always think Lucas was made for me. Whatever we go through together will be a team effort and he and I will be supportive in every way."

"I know he will take care of you. When your mom and sister died, I thought I was going to lose my mind. There were times when I had to take long walks up at the cabin, missing them so much. I tried to keep it together. Pain has a way of moving in and not letting go."

"I felt that way too and finally came to terms with it. After a while, I realized what they would want was for me to carry on without them. I remember

Jen complaining that I never cried and didn't care. I held it all in until I met Marie and Lucas. They helped me see it was okay to cry. I don't think my mother wanted me to carry that pain with me for so long."

"I hold my daughters a little tighter now. I never want to take them for granted. They are growing so fast and I miss listening to those sounds of laughter when they were younger. I am so blessed to have them in my life."

"I am glad you have them."

"Chapman is my only brother. When he was young, he had Caryn by his side all the time. I can't remember a time when they were without family. She was such a delight to have around. She wanted me to be her maid of honor at their wedding. I never had a sister and getting close to Caryn was so good for me. After Chap settled into marriage, he was always holding her and telling her he loved her. Their love was something I wished I had when I was married."

"I loved that they had so much affection for each other."

Lilly pulled a wrapped book from her bag and opened it in front of Bailee's curious eyes.

"I found this on our parent's bookshelf after they passed away. It had been sitting there unread for quite a while. It's not the title that impressed me, *Songbirds of the West*. It was what was inside that caught my breath. Tell me what you think."

She handed it gently to her. Bailee's eyes lit up when it fell open at the center. A small rose lay flat and four smaller pansies below it. In the lower margin was penciled, *One day I will have many children to love.*

"This must have been before she was married."

"Your mother had so much love to give. She would be so proud of you."

"Yes, but now I am only one daughter," she sighed.

"You are worth more than that. You are a beautiful person inside and out."

"Thank you, Lilly."

"This is what I want for you and Lucas. You have found that same love and will build it over time to become deep and trustworthy. Your father taught you by example. Take what your parents gave you and run with it. I have no doubt you will have a happy life."

Bailee took one of the sketches from her book and handed it to her.

"I always thought of you as a flower. Maybe it was because of your name. This makes me think of you. The flowers by the lake bring back great memories of us."

Bailee hugged her aunt and took to heart her kind words. They talked for a while about the fun times their families had over the years. It was obvious that laughter had returned to their lives. It felt good to smile about the past and put sadness behind them. Bailee knew her aunt was going to miss her. The good times they had together and all the intimate talks they shared helped make good moments happen for Bailee. Lilly came by not only to say goodbye to her only niece, but to share her feelings about what their family had been through. She watched Bailee become a grown woman making decisions on her own. Love was evident and Lilly was proud of how far she had come.

"Never forget how much I love you, Bailee," she added as she descended the stairs.

At the other end of town, Brad and his new wife were sitting in Chap's living room. Bailee's art hung over his fireplace. He let them know about his daughter's move.

"Sounds like she has a wonderful life ahead of her," his wife admired.

"And how are you doing now, old Chap?" asked Brad.

"I could learn a lot from Bailee. I wish I had her bravery."

"You do, Chap. You are so much better than you have been."

"Bailee made me that way."

"You did it. Give yourself some credit for making peace with Caryn's passing."

"I don't where I would be without Bailee here. I know she needs to go, but it stills makes me anxious. That's my foible," he stated comically.

"You will always have us," assured Brad. It sounds like there may be a wedding in her future. That's a good thing to look forward to."

"It is and I've always wanted to be a grandfather. Bailee would make a good mother."

Chap could see so much waiting for his daughter. In the past, he may not have been able to handle letting her go so far away. There were so many bad things that could have happened to her, but he also saw many good possibilities for her. It was good to have friends that could see reality a little clearer than he could. Chap was getting better at seeing his glass half full. Brad and his wife always left him in good spirits.

Bailee was finally ready and brought her luggage downstairs. Nan was waiting with a gift in her hand.

"You are going to have a good time living in France. I know I did when I was young. I want to give you this."

"What is this? Is this you when you were young?"

"Yes. It's one of the most memorable times of my life. I was encouraged to model. I could travel and look pretty while painting and selling art. It took me to some beautiful places in my life. I just knew being a model wasn't the life for me. Color and paint will always be my first passion."

"Who took this picture?"

"Giuseppe. It was the last day we shared together."

"I can't take this. This is too special."

"That is all behind me now. I want you to have it. It will inspire you to paint," she quipped.

Bailee was honored to receive it. She could see a love of France inside of Nan and a part of her wanted to go back to live out the rest of her years.

"I will take good care of it."

"I know you will. Take lots of pictures and send them to me."

"I've treasured our time together. Thank you for believing in me."

"It was like having a daughter of my own." Nan was getting emotional. "Well, look at me. I am not going to fall apart when you leave. These are happy tears."

She pulled a lace handkerchief from her handbag and dabbed her cheek. A taxi parked in front of the gallery waiting for Bailee. One last hug and she was gone.

When Bailee arrived at the airport drop-off, her father surprised her.

"Dad! What are you doing here?"

"I forgot something. Your mother wanted to you to have this when you found true love."

He placed a necklace around her. She touched and admired it.

"She's had kept this since high school. She bought it for a special occasion when we were young. That was when she discovered she wanted to spend her life with me. I have been holding on to it all these years. Now it's yours."

"I love it. This really means a lot."

He stood there not knowing what to say or do next.

"Call when you get there. Let me know you made it okay, he muttered.

"I will."

Chap took a long look at her and turned to leave. Bailee put her hand on his shoulder and stopped him.

"Dad, Lilly said that you and Mom were a good example for me to have a good life. Especially when it comes to love. I want to say thank you for that."

"I did my best."

"You did better than that."

Chap kissed her cheek and gave a wave. With butterflies in her stomach, she was ready to join Lucas.

The flight felt longer and sleep became the comfort to curb her anxiety. It all became real when she touched down. Filing through the mass of passengers to baggage claim, she knew Lucas was waiting for her close by. Some of her things had been shipped to Marie's home. After dragging her bags to the exit, she saw Lucas next to Marie. Dropping everything, she ran into his arms.

Marie interjected, "Don't I get hug too? Or do I have to wait until tomorrow."

"Oh, I am so glad you are both here! It seems like forever!"

"Normandy awaits you, young lady. Shall we take all of this to my car?"

Lucas hoisted her things and followed them towards the parking area.

Bailee knew it wasn't the penultimate chapter of her story. What lay in store for her was just the beginning.

Chapter 22

We Came Together For Jen

The ride back was pleasant. She recalled the first time she made the trip to see Marie on the coast. Thoughts stirred in her mind, never imagining she would actually call it home. As they approached the west bound road, Marie turned right. She was not taking them to her cottage in Normandy but stopped at the train station instead.

"Why are we here?" Bailee puzzled.

"You and Lucas are getting on the train."

"I thought we were all going to your place," she said confused.

Lucas gave her a short answer, trying not to reveal too much.

"There's a good reason why we're here and that is all I'm going to say."

"Don't worry, dear. I will take your things to my home and see you later. Now, go with Lucas."

Marie knew exactly what Lucas' plans were.

Bailee conceded, "I'm okay with that. It will be nice to see Henri's cottage again. I love that little place."

After Marie left, Bailee and Lucas waited for a few minutes until the sound of their train announced itself. They let go of each other and stepped on board. Lucas kept expressing how glad he was that Bailee was part of his Parisian community. It was a dream coming true. Two souls discovering each other, confident that they found exactly what their hearts were searching for. Lucas kept his customary affection by holding Bailee's hand throughout the train ride. He hoped she wasn't suspecting anything unusual about their detour.

"Please disembark to the exits, *s'il vous plait!"* the ticket man shouted.

They stepped out and began down the side road.

Bailee breathed in deeply and exhaled. "I love this walk to your home. It's something I could get used to."

"I'm glad to hear you say that." Lucas did his best to keep quiet.

"So, what is the real reason we are not going to Marie's?"

"Remember when we met and you didn't like me asking so many questions? You thought I was prying."

"You were."

"Right, I was annoying to quote you, and right now it seems like you can't be surprised."

He was swinging her hand back and forth and smiling, trying to contain his excitement.

"There's a surprise? What could you possibly surprise me with? You've already done so much for me."

Lucas looked up and smiled. As the road passed through the trees, they could glimpse Lucas' land. It was cozily nestled as before, but Bailee noticed it was not quite the same. After all, she had only been there once before near dusk. The cottage appeared larger. She could smell lavender and sweet-smelling flowers planted along the walk. Newly painted window and door frames invited her forward.

“What is this? What have you done?” she marveled.

“I made a few changes while you were away. It made the hours go by faster, anticipating our new home together.”

“Oh, I loved it the way it was. You didn’t have to go to all that trouble for me.”

“It was no trouble at all. I did this for us. Come, let’s see the inside.”

She opened the door and stood there, amazed. It did not look like the cottage she remembered. The old fireplace was still there, but the bed was gone and a second chair sat in its place. The kitchen wall was also removed and new windows added daylight. She noticed more cabinets and an enlarged island with a soapstone top. She slowly ran her hand across it. The home she fell in love in still warmed her heart.

“Oh, Lucas! You will love cooking in here!”

“This isn’t all I added. Check out these new rooms,” he pointed with pride.

He had expanded the bathroom and added a clawfoot tub below the window. Next to it was the primary bedroom, accented by wooden French doors leading to the garden. Curtains alongside them touched the floor, puddling casually, adding to its comfort. The other room was smaller with a small bed and dresser. A multi-colored braided area rug lay in the middle. As she admired it, Lucas asked Bailee to decide how she would use the spare room. He guessed it as an art studio. He enjoyed watching her take the tour. As she returned to the living room, she spoke.

"This isn't the same place, Lucas. It's so beautiful!"

"I didn't want to change anything about Henri's home but now that you are here, this is going to be home for us. By the way, I have to thank Marie. She helped out and kept it very quiet."

"She knew about this? She did a good job with your secret."

"I want to take you to one more surprise. Come with me to the garden." He took her hand as she tried to imagine what else he could show.

"This is a special place. I built this one from my heart."

"Why is there another small cottage there?" she asked.

"That home is for your father, Chapman. If he ever wants to live here closer to the ones he loves, he can make this his forever home."

On one side a large oak spread its branches, begging children to climb and swing on. For a moment, Bailee could see her father living there, playing with his grandchildren, and visiting often. Her father's happiness always meant a lot to her after all they went through.

"What if he doesn't want to live here?" she wondered.

"Well, he can stay here when he visits. But I want him to live near you. We have each other, but a daughter will always need her father. Henri taught me that."

Between the homes, white fencing embraced a lush garden. Just outside the enclosure, varied fruit trees and grape vines were planted. Inside, flowers were mixed with vegetables and herbs. Tomatoes hung heavily from their vines and haricots verts which are green beans, were climbing up their poles. Because of Lucas' love of zucchini flowers in his dishes, several plants sprawled near other summer vegetables. The old pump still sat where Henri installed it to draw water from the well. It still worked. Lucas had no reason to take it out and kept it rustic. Bailee walked into the garden and sampled a juicy tomato and then opened a pod of peas.

"I don't have the words for all I'm feeling right now, except that I am grateful to be here with you." she said softly.

"I missed you so much waiting until you came home. Doing this for you helped me to survive until you were back in my arms again. I'm glad you like it."

"I love it."

Lucas put his arms around her, happy to see her unwrap the present he waited so long to open. He had thought about what she might want in a home, about her father, and all of their losses. For so long, he put everything into his café. He had searched for love and almost found it in Monique. He did his best to get over losing his beloved, Henri. Mingling Bailee's story with his, they were paired perfectly to give love a fighting chance, victorious over pain. Lucas could never cover it all perfectly, but he wanted life to be pleasant for her as she let her loved ones rest. The home would have an abundance of love and good food. It would be filled with the sounds of happy children along with tears and disagreements. They would slumber in a soft bed together, holding each other, gaining warmth.

Cool winters and warm summers were to come and go each year. Lucas could see it all with Bailee next to him. He walked her around the edges of his land, talking about its features and future improvements he planned.

As the evening cooled, the two of them gathered some ripened produce and washed it at the pump. Inside he taught her how to start a small fire, then both began preparing their meal. Lucas was happy to slow down and include her as they conversed and laughed. Memories of her first night in the cottage were relived.

She nudged him, "Do you still sing while you cook?"

"Of course! What shall I sing tonight?"

"Something Italian."

Night settled in and the air chilled. They stood in front of the fire until Bailee suggested she needed to sleep. It was already past midnight.

Lucas, can we sleep in front of the fire like before?"

"Yes. Can I ask you something?" He arranged some blankets and pillows. "Will you be happy here? I mean, instead of a fancy place in the city?"

She looked into his eyes and exposed her most honest thoughts.

"Lucas, this is where your heart is. I only want to be where you are. It makes me the happiest."

The melody of the fire crackling helped Bailee sleep quickly. The end of one fine day would be the start of many to follow.

A fresh morning and coffee started their day as they strolled to the station. The plan had been for Bailee to live with Marie before settling in at the cottage as Lucas' wife. Normandy looked prettier than when she left it. She noticed fewer travelers. Foliage had changed its colors and the river ran a quiet gray. Marie's home always smelled like a warm oven. The two loved being together especially in the evening. Her outdoor chairs pointed toward the setting sun and did not disappoint until the clouds rolled in. Wine and warm conversations by the fire was just what she needed to feel at home in the country.

Weeks had passed when Bailee called her father again.

"Dad, how are you?"

"I'm well. I got your letter. How is France?"

"Wonderful. Lucas remodeled his home and it's so lovely. You should see it. Dad, I want to send you a ticket to come visit. Will you come?"

"Oh, I don't know. I've never traveled that far away. Is there something you want to tell me, something important?" he hinted.

"Well, not yet. I do want you to come stay with me. You will love it here and you can meet Marie. We have had the best of times along the coast."

Chap had been practicing coming out of his comfort zone and stepping back from anxiety to manage his fears. He thought about what he might learn from Marie about his precious Jen. Losing touch with his oldest daughter was a hard loss and it was time to focus on better times.

"You can be so convincing, Bailee."

"Great. I'll send you a ticket with the date on it. I can't wait to see you again, Dad."

Chapman was feeling more positive those days. As the months moved by, therapy helped get his life in order. Bailee could see it and thought it would be a good time to spring the news about him living near her. It might be a big move but Bailee would be persuasive.

Brad began spending more time with his wife than Chap. She was pregnant with twins. Chap realized he was getting along fine on his own and socialized more. He attempted dating a woman who became more of a friend than a love interest. That was a big step for him. The invitation to go to France held his attention. It was something he began looking forward to. His first thought was to hold back and not accept her offer. But he could hear the encouraging words of his counselor telling him that he was more than ready to take progressive steps to recovery. He recognized that it was really an opportunity to spread his wings and show himself that he could live again.

Bailee would spend several days each week with Lucas at the café and then his home. Sometimes, Marie would join them. She wanted them to get to know each other better without being a third wheel. When Bailee and Marie talked about the visit of her father, Marie could feel her family growing. When her son, Jason died, she felt alone. She had no living family around except neighbors who would take care of her in if she needed to talk or cry on a willing shoulder. Things slowly improved. Meeting Jen at the time that she did, made her new family connections possible. There was a closeness she didn't remember ever having. When she was married to her ex-husband, she thought the three of them were a complete family and it was all she needed until things changed and tragedy struck. She lived her life without imaging that anyone could bring that much love to her and claim her as family. What a blessing it was to have met such a beautiful soul in Jen and know her family. The appearance of Bailee into Marie's life was like having Jen around again.

The time finally came when Chap landed in France, passport and all. Experiencing travel for the first time, he was quietly aware of his surroundings. It was a new adventure and he would take it in with Bailee by his side. She expected her father to fall in love with France the way she did. She wanted him to see it all. She would take him to dinner, have coffee together and visit memorable sights. It brought out a side of Chap that his daughter had been waiting to see. He talked about his own plans for the future and new things he wanted to explore. Of course, dating was not part of his plan at the moment. He realized that more people had come into his life. As he aged, he wanted to be sure not to let special moments pass him by. His heart softened seeing his daughter in love. He remembered that feeling and missed it. He understood that he had been loved by the best.

Marie expected their arrival. It was time for Chap to meet the woman who changed his daughter and made a large difference in her tumultuous world. He wasn't sure what to expect entering Marie's home. His experience with therapists gave him insight on how she might carry herself when she was around him. She was nothing like any of the counselors he talked to. Totally surprised, Chap found her pleasant and hospitable.

She welcomed them into her home and Chap sat quietly. Marie thought she should loosen up the conversation by offering some wine or food. Neither said no to that. He quickly relaxed and happy, enjoying the light conversation. Marie knew he had questions about Jen and what she went through while in New York.

"Chap, how was your trip?" Marie asked.

"It was good. I'm glad we had a layover to break up the long hours in coach."

"I'm happy you came to visit our beautiful country. France has a way of making us appreciate the love and food we have."

"Bailee made sure to take me to some of her favorite places to eat. Café Henri was a wonderful place to have breakfast."

"I believe your girl is now French. She knows so much about our food and wine since she has been with Lucas,' Marie complemented.

"Everything is so delicious, I'm sure I'll notice my jeans fitting a little tighter from all the butter," Bailee joked.

Marie sat back and smiled at the good time they were having until Chap spoke.

"Marie, I want to thank you for being there for Jen when she really needed a friend. Your caring demeanor is appreciated. I was able to get help with my own loss."

"Would you like me to tell you about her and what we talked about?'

"I would love that."

Marie started with her own story, including abuse and her son, Jason. She pulled out pictures of the three of them during happier times and what made her want to be a counselor. Before she got her license, she heard too many stories about abused women who died by the hand of a controlling personality. Some made it out alive and she used her own time and resources helping others break free. When she met Jen, she observed similar behaviors. In their conversations, Jen wanted to imitate Marie in helping others in her situation.

Chap leaned in and asked sincerely, "You said you thought your son was dangerous. Was he capable of more than just controlling Jen?"

"I never want to pin it on anyone who has a child, but Jason was taking on the persona of his father. He was angry that he left us and he never even acknowledged him, not once. In my heart, I feared for Jen's life."

It was hard to fathom that Jason could have become a murderer to get what he wanted. He was already showing signs of what could have been. Before Jen died in the 9/11 attacks, she hadn't completely fallen into the clutches of Jason. She was smart enough to get away and was on her way to having a fuller life without fear.

"I hold no resentment towards you, Marie. I am sad for your loss as well," Chap thought how both of them held similar emotions.

"Thank you."

Marie couldn't help herself and rose from her chair to hug Chap. As she did, she whispered, "I am here if you ever need a good friend."

Chap took hold of Bailee's hand and squeezed. It was the closure he needed. Those women were his family and nothing could break that apart. They enjoyed stories about France and good time to come.

Lucas was completing inventory and hated to miss out on Chap's visit. He worked hard so that he could spend more time with Bailee. Soon he would meet the man who brought his daughter into the world. Later that evening, he arrived tired and spent. That did not stop him from running into Chap's arms, greeting him in a Parisian fashion. Marie served him some wine and reheated the meal they shared.

"Lucas, I think you and food are the best of friends. Every time I cook something, you go for it with full force," Marie chuckled.

"Yes, food is a celebration to the palate."

Chap sat back and watched. Lucas was a happy man surrounded by family and laughter. This was something the young man had missed out on for so long. Having Henri in his life was good, but in Normandy sat a complete family just like his great-grandfather had in his day.

After two weeks in France, Chap returned to California. He too was caught up in the ambiance of Paris and the newfound family he now called his own. After a year, Chap decided to move to France and live in the cottage Lucas built. During that time, Lucas and Bailee married. Each year they watched the news about 9/11 to honor those who lost their lives, it was a moment to reflect on what they had when Jen was alive.

The next ten years after the Twin Towers collapsed, Bailee, Marie, and Chap had not visited New York until they received a letter from the Mayor. By that time, she had two school-age sons who loved following in their father's footsteps. When the letter came, Bailee waited to read it with her whole family.

"Why would the Mayor send us a letter?" Chap asked.

"I don't know. Let's open in and find out."

Her heart beat a little faster as she tore into the envelope.

To Bailee and Chapman Collins,

We want to say how sorry we are that you lost someone you loved in that heinous crime against humanity on September 11. We hope your family is coping well.

The reason for this letter is to let you know that we are starting a memorial service at Ground Zero for those who have left us in death and those who gave it their all to save others.

Jen Bryce Collins is being honored for her unselfish donation to the Community for Abused Children and Adults. Before her death, she gave most of her money to this organization and related her own story of abuse and fear. She wrote us a touching letter stating why she was being so generous. A copy has been saved in our archives.

They had no clue about money or any donations. It was a shock to discover and heartwarming to hear. They were in suspense as Bailee unfolded Jen's letter.

My friends,

I want to dedicate this donation to those who became trapped or lost their lives to anyone who thought control and abuse would benefit them and their victims. I am no longer a victim, thanks to the loving and caring hand of Marie Thomas. I thought the person I loved was someone who would take care of me and love me. He fooled me into thinking we had a future together. Marie warned me that his intentions were potentially dangerous to me. I got away safe after he hit me in my own apartment during a jealous rage. Marie came into my life at the perfect time and I thank her for taking me under her wing and inviting me to her city in France. This is where I am going to make my home. Most of all, she helped me love my father again. Getting away from what terrified me brought out the woman that was hiding inside. It would have gotten worse. Even though a part of me loved him, I needed to free myself from his hooks. I realized it was not my fault. Many times I tried to help with his temper, but he refused in anger. That anger was always shoved back in my face. He thought he succeeded by blaming me for his own actions.

So, I am giving some of what I got for my business to a wonderful organization that works hard to rescue and save lives. I read stories of women like me who gained their life back after abuse and became CEO's, mothers, and successful humans. I want them to be free to choose as I am. I have visited the shelters and people in need who thank me for what support I have within me and I have given the greatest gift of all, love.

Jen Bryce Collins

Bailee, you are invited to New York at Ground Zero to receive an honor for Jen's caring generosity. We would also like you to give a speech about what she meant to you. We hope you can attend. You are welcome to bring Chapman, Marie Thomas and the rest of your family.

September 11, 2011 at 9 in the morning.

We are so happy to give you this news.

Take care, The Mayor of New York City

Overwhelmed, smiles filled the room. It was something they would not say no to. They immediately made preparations to fly to New York. This was their time to stick together without sadness but to celebrate a gifted human being. Jen deserved the honor and her family was proud of her for who she became and what she had done.

Chapter 23

I Will Remember You

Bailee and her family arrived in New York in the morning. They toured the blocks where the towers used to stand. In 2003, the Lower Manhattan Corporation had overseen the revitalization of the downtown after 9/11. A design was chosen that would be a permanent memorial for the World Trade Center site. A competition received 5,201 entries from 63 countries. A 13-person jury looked for the best way to honor the victims by speaking to their families to provide a space for healing and reflection. The Memorial opened September 11, 2011.

They were impressed by the two pools, each nearly one acre in size where the former towers stood. The sound of the largest manmade waterfalls in North America, fell 30 feet into the square basin, masked sounds of city life. From there, the water dropped another 20 feet and disappeared into a smaller opening. More than 400 white oak trees filled the Memorial plaza, chosen because they were native to all of the 9/11 crash sites: New York City, Arlington, Virginia, and Somerset County, Pennsylvania.

In October 2001, recovery workers discovered a severely damaged Callery Pear tree at Ground Zero. After removing it and nursing it back to life, the tree became known as the Survivor Tree. It was returned in 2010 as a symbol of resilience and perseverance.

Visitors searched the southwestern quadrant of the Memorial plaza, dedicated in honor of all who became sick and died from exposure to toxic materials and dust in the aftermath. Its pathway was flanked by six large stone monoliths, each inlaid with the towers steel, symbolizing strength through adversity.

The Glade opened May 30, 2019, marking the 17th anniversary of the official end of the recovery period.

Bailee found Jen and Jason's names on the stone memorial block and gathered her family together to remember that horrific day with tears. Soon after, Bailee was called to the platform to talk about the sister she loved. Slightly nervous, she reminded herself what this means to her and her family.

"Thank you everyone for coming to this special day. Today is about honoring those we lost and loved," the emcee said from the podium.

He went on to talk about the Memorial and some of the facts that led up to that day. After speaking to the crowd for a few minutes, he introduced Bailee.

"At this time, I would like to invite Bailee Carter Laurent, whose sister Jen, was killed in Tower 1. Bailee, please."

Bailee had a few notes with her, but most of what she was going to say would come from her heart. All was quiet and she could hear her heart beating. She took a deep breath and began.

"I am pleased to be here to honor a wonderful woman who made a difference in my life. We were

sisters and the best of friends. Even though we were different, we could understand each other. Our closeness held us up despite what we went through as teenagers. Our mother left us when we were young from heart disease. It was hard for us to accept, but we knew she loved us very much. Jen was exceptionally close to our mother. They had a relationship that was meaningful and precious. Maybe it was because she was the firstborn and had spent more time together. Jen would send me letters about special family moments. Recalling those good times made missing her difficult for me and my dad. My father wanted his first child to be a daughter. He already named her before he knew what she was going to be. At her birth, she was Jen. Not Jenny, not Jennifer, just Jen. We never called her anything else. As children, we laughed all the time and played with our parents. When Dad had to focus on helping Mom during her illness, Jen realized the joy ended and a loneliness set inside her.

When she moved to New York, my father let her live her own life. Jen became successful at business but also held a deep, dark secret. She was a victim of abuse and felt trapped. She found help, being relieved of what she was experiencing. Before coming home, she began supporting others who were just like her. Jen loved the city of New York and she loved its people more. The day Jen died in that tower; we were broken apart. There was so much more to know about her but it was too late. Today, I am here to thank her for how much she cared about those who felt just like her. Her generosity has touched and saved many lives with her story and donation. I was told there are some in the audience that were friends with Jen and thanked her for her support.

Marie Thomas, who is here today, lost her son in the same tower. Jason was my sister's business partner. Marie sheltered my sister in her arms and helped her on her way to being freed from her chains. Even though he died in Tower 1, Marie loved her son. Jen will always be missed. As a family, we have put it to rest and focus on how blessed we are to have known such a gifted woman, sister, and daughter.

I know many of us here are still struggling to make sense of it all. Maybe some of us will never get over the pain. Despite all that, we all knew someone who was special and loved. That is the memory that can never be removed from our hearts and thoughts. This memorial will be a remembrance of what could have been for the victims. I am grateful to have shared my younger years with someone who loved me and who I called, sister. Jen willingly gave up her success for others. She was truly unselfish. My heart goes out to each of you honoring your loved ones. I want to thank my father Chapman and Marie Thomas for their loving support. My husband, Lucas Henri Laurent and our sons, Gabriele and Benoit. I will now read a letter written to Jen Bryce Collins.

Each time I think of you, I think of beautiful things. Flowers in springtime draped over an Italian balcony. Two souls laughing together and sharing what could be. When I visit Normandy where lush fields are painted with their colors, I picture you there with me. You sit next to me and tell me that you finally feel free from all of the unwanted pain you suffered. These are my thoughts wishing you were here with me. Since you went away, I have travelled and walked streets and roads, wishing I could see your face. I remember when we were very young, you thought it would be better to run away together. You had a plan and it would all be okay because you would keep me safe. Why did you have that thought? What was hurting inside? I knew in time; you would share what was torturing you and why you had to say goodbye.

You were taken from us too soon and after all these years, I still miss you and what you would have become if you survived. Jen, the most precious memories of us are set here in my mind. I read your letters; some I know by heart. Each time I read them, it's like you're here. I'm so glad you saved each one. They are like gold to me and I will keep them safe.

Even though you are not here, I will always love you. My children will learn about you and your kindness to strangers, how you liked to walk the streets of New York greeting different people, having tea with the elderly women at the park. There are so many stories that can be told about your loving heart.

Now your family honors a woman who was brave and found strength only some of us wish we had. Thank you for being a part of me. You are forever in my heart.

Bailee stepped off the stage and the audience applauded at her moving tribute. In the distance among the crowd, was Diane Combs, sitting in her wheelchair beside her daughter. When Diane heard of Jen having tea with an elderly woman, she realized Jen was the woman who had given her the jewelry. She touched her daughter's hand and began to cry. Jen's memory was living in the hearts of those she touched. All were moved by others who took their turn memorializing their loved ones.

When the family returned to France, they placed some of the pictures of their trip in a special album to review from time to time. Bailee's sons loved spending time outside with Chap. They were at his home almost everyday and Chap had dinner with them each night. Living in France transformed him more than he expected. His life felt full and purposeful.

Everyone's life changed for the better. Even though the past years were hard, happiness pushed it aside to help a family come together. Chap and Marie have a close relationship without romance and have become the best of friends. Chap voiced how he would never find love again, but her supportive friendship came at the right time. Marie could only say, "I understand. You will always have my loyalty as a friend."

Nan occasionally visits when she can. Age slows her down but that doesn't stop her from enjoying trips to her favorite place in Normandy.

The years are good to Bailee. She gave her sons a good start and to this day, they still love the art of food and cooking with their father. Bailee is a good wife and mother living out the rest of her days in the peaceful pocket of France.

As you enter the warmth of her loving home, a glass vase sits filled with fresh flowers. Bailee places it where the light reflects its beautiful shape and color, filled with love and happiness. It is a reminder of Jen while alive, thanks to those who loved her. The glass vase now takes on new meaning. Special people are loved for who they are on the inside. Beautiful souls are those who give everything they have to anyone needing love. Bailee never doubted it. For her, life is the best it has ever been. Her memoirs are dedicated to the two parents who loved their little girls.

For Chapman and Caryn Collins

The Glass Vase

Other Books By Annette Stephenson

Divided Mountain

The Landscaper's Wife

The Tree at Lindley Park

The Other Side of Brook

The Shoe Box

The Last Memory

The Many Colors of Poetry

Annette Marie Stephenson

Made in the USA
Monee, IL
13 May 2023

33436298R10154